Remember
I'M YOURS

A PREQUEL TO DIESEL ROSE

VANESSA LUISA

Remember I'm Yours: A Prequel to Diesel Rose
Editor: Ellie McLove at My Brother's Editor
Proofreader: Emily A. Lawrence
Formatter: Champagne Book Design
Cover Photographer: Daniel Jaems (Paperback Model)
Cover Design: ©KiWi Cover Design Co.

ISBN: 978-0-6450535-4-8

This book contains mature content.

Remember I'm Yours: A Prequel to Diesel Rose

From the moment I gazed into his melancholic onyx eyes, *I knew he would be mine.*

Elijah Diesel isn't just my gorgeous, older, mysterious obsession, he's also the lead vocalist of an up-and-coming alternative rock band due to take the world by storm.

He wanted nothing to do with me.
Yet he kept coming back.
And I let him.

And now, only one thing is certain.
This won't be the end of us…
Because it's only just our beginning.

NOTE: This is a 25,000-word prequel novella for DIESEL ROSE.
The story concludes in DIESEL ROSE.

For all the monsters under the bed who end up saving lives with their dark poetry...

And to Mamma, Nonna, and Nonno,
My love for you all is infinite.
<3

"Things are sweeter when they're lost."

F. SCOTT FITZGERALD, *THE BEAUTIFUL AND DAMNED*

"I said maybe
You're gonna be the one that saves me
And after all
You're my wonderwall."

OASIS, 'WONDERWALL'

Playlist

"Scary Love"—The Neighbourhood

"SUPERMODEL"—Måneskin

"Brooklyn Baby"—Lana Del Ray

"Tell Me The Truth"—Two Feet

"Wonderwall"—Oasis

"Beetlejuice chill"—Life After Youth

"Baby Came Home 2 / Valentines"—The Neighbourhood

"Enemy (with JD)"—Imagine Dragons, JID, Arcane, League of Legends

"True Rocker"—Monster Truck, Dee Snider

"Triggered"—Chase Atlantic

"IN NOME DEL PADRE"—Måneskin

"Flawless"—The Neighbourhood

"Cherry"—Lana Del Ray

"Like A God"—Lia Marie Johnson

"Devil's Advocate"—The Neighbourhood

"Scary People"—Georgi Kay

"Love Become Law"—The Cherry Truck Band, Black Stone Cherry, Monster Truck

Remember
I'M YOURS

A PREQUEL TO DIESEL ROSE

Chapter
ONE

Rosalia

I think I have a boy crush. Okay, let me rephrase that, I *do* have a boy crush.

One of my favorite things to do at a quarter to midnight whenever I can't sleep is scrapbook. My mom is a hairdresser downtown and always brings home old magazines clients flick through so I can cut out whatever I like. At first, it gave me the heebie-jeebies touching magazines a dozen other women (and possibly men too) had touched, but now I guess I'm over it.

Tonight was supposed to be like any other night. Flip through the magazines, cut out aesthetically pleasing vintage pieces with my pink diamanté scissors, and slap them in my scrapbook. Except, tonight *isn't* like any other night, it's different, because my mom didn't only bring home old editions of *Vogue* and *Harper's Bazaar* in a white plastic bag that's laced with holes. There's also something else.

Rolling Stone magazine.

And the good thing is, it's the latest edition.

May.

She's never brought a *Rolling Stone* magazine home for me before, and I wonder if she accidentally got it from the barber section at her work. I wasn't going to look through it, but I did, and *God,* how grateful I am that I did.

It's the first page I randomly opened on.

Page twelve.

And I haven't dared look away since.

Dark-gray eyes, the lightest shade of onyx stare back at me. They're the kind of eyes that are so cold, they should scare you. Instead, they have a sense of sugary thrill flooding my body. They're devilish. Wolfish. Everything my parents warned me about. *And everything I crave.*

My heart skips a beat because he's the most beautiful man I've seen, in a dark and edgy kind of way. A deadly piercing gaze. Perfectly high cheekbones. Thin full lips that remind me of James Dean's.

Everything about the black-and-white picture

of this man leaning against a barbed-wire fence intrigues me. His punk-inspired leather jacket with silvery spikes around his shoulders and safety pins by the edges. The destroyed white tee underneath. His distressed black jeans. Those unlaced black Doc Martens with a single white broken love heart on the side of the left one, almost as if it's been stitched.

It feels like there's a story behind those white Band-Aids wrapped around some of his fingers that he has looped above his head in the wire. I'm fascinated by the ink on his hands, the ones more visible like the skull, serpent, and roman numerals, and I instantly wonder if he has more.

Why is he making my heart go so funny?

I like the way he's looking at the camera with furrowed brows, a mixture between broody and motionless, making it seem like he just doesn't give a damn. Like life has done a number on him.

I stare a little too long at the thin black eyeliner around his eyes. I always thought eyeliner was for girls, but seeing it on him, I know I've been wrong… *wow, it's really hot.*

I brush the pad of my finger over his face, almost intimidated at first, as I wonder if his eyes are really that dark or are instead a dark cocoa brown. Maybe it's just the dark ink of the page tricking me? Maybe.

Beneath his photo, a white cursive font reads:

The true hatesick up-and-coming sinner of Manhattan;
Elijah Diesel.

Elijah.

"Elijah," I murmur to myself, wanting to get used to the name on my tongue. "Elijah Diesel."

He seems a few years older than me, okay, *a lot* older. Ten years my senior at the least, and although I so desperately want to read all of the little text surrounding the picture, I kind of want to make my own impression of the guy.

After chewing my bottom lip for the longest time, I cut out his picture, being careful to make it perfect, and stick it on a new page in my scrapbook.

Elijah Diesel

I write in permanent marker as a title on the page, and then I draw four little black hearts.

A little lower down, toward the bottom of my page, I write all my feelings out with my heart beating a million miles per second.

Right now I'm looking at you for the first time, and I think I'm going to get addicted to you. I want to know everything about you, Elijah. Or should I call you Diesel?

Butterflies take over my stomach and I can't help just how deeply my cheeks burn. I roll over on my bed to my back and cover my mouth, softening my giddy giggles while New York's silvery moonlight merges with my warm yellow wall sconces.

"Stop being so foolish, Rosalia Philips," I whisper to myself. "He's just some hot rocker."

But I know he's much more than that.

He's the first person who's managed to make me crack a smile through my midnight blues.

The first man who makes me feel a funny type of way just staring at his picture.

The only one I think I'll get lost in forever, until he's staring right back at me.

Whoa.

I settle down and stare up at my ceiling, a seventeen-year-old girl trying to rebel from the world as she knows it, second by second.

Who are you, Elijah Diesel?

Exactly where can I find you?

And why does my heart beat so crazy for you?

It's been a month, and my mom hasn't brought home the next edition of *Rolling Stone* magazine for me.

I tried buying the latest edition before school this morning, but the damn newsagent had just sold out. I knew a couple more in the area, but I would have been late for the last day of eleventh grade before summer, so I promised myself I'd check out the other newsstands after school.

The anticipation has been killing me all day because as much as I know I can just search up Elijah Diesel on my phone, there's so much more thrill in turning a page and seeing him instead.

It's just after three o'clock when I step into the convenience store by my school.

The older guy behind the counter takes one look at my wavy blonde hair, my cropped white shirt, and pink-and-white plaid skirt and scoffs, "Kids these days."

With a clenched jaw, I ball my fists but continue walking to the section of the store I know all the hotshot magazines are, no matter how deeply the man's words hurt me.

I'm not even the worst of my generation. I swear, I'm not. First, I don't relate to my generation. At all. Second, I've never had a sip of alcohol. Never smoked. Done drugs in the bathroom. Hell, I've never even kissed a guy in my entire life.

I'm just a seventeen-year-old virgin who loves short plaid skirts and knee-high socks. I'm not hurting anybody, so to hell with this guy.

Why don't you fix your flickering lightbulbs, popcorn ceiling, and grossly stained carpet instead, dude?

I almost do a happy dance on the spot when the

new edition of *Rolling Stone* stares back at me. It's the last one left. I grin and snatch it from the stand at record speed, then I actually start bouncing.

Yes. Yes. Yes.

Just as I begin flipping through it, wanting to see if I can see a glimpse of Elijah Diesel before I buy it, the man behind the counter clears his throat.

My breath slows and I don't like the glare he shoots my way. "Aye, blondie, this isn't a library. You want to read the magazine, you buy it and you get the hell out of my store."

Rude.

Narrowing my eyes, I slap a twenty-dollar bill on the counter and practically run out of the store, not caring about the change. My mom would kill me if she knew, but once won't make a difference, *right*?

Rushing down the street, I wait until I'm on the next block before I come to a slow by my bus stop. Even though I live in Brooklyn, I go to school in Manhattan. Don't ask me why, but my father—one of the most respected neurosurgeons in the city—wanted it that way. And that way it is.

Leaning against the bus shelter, I couldn't be more ecstatic as I slip my schoolbag between my feet and carefully turn each page of the magazine. New York's slightly warm breeze kisses my skin and blows my waves, giving me hope of a beautiful summer approaching.

But that hope slowly shrivels up when I go through the entire magazine, never seeing a photo of Elijah Diesel once.

My heart drops.

No.

No. No. No.

He has to be in here. *He's got to!*

I go over the magazine a second time, then a third, and by the fourth time I'm groaning. I seriously feel like slamming it right in the trash can, so devastated that I waited an entire month for nothing.

"It can't be." I sigh, shutting my eyes just as the bus pulls up. "How can he not be in it?"

It's just my luck. Something like this was bound to happen to me.

I just wasted twenty dollars. That idiot back in the store will probably wipe his mouth with it after devouring a greasy cheeseburger.

Ickkk.

For me, it isn't just false hope, it's giving in to the fantasy of Elijah Diesel slipping away from my very fingers. I so desperately craved another photo of him to put in my scrapbook. One I can stare at whenever I don't feel all right, just like I did for the past month, but now I feel like a fool for doing so.

You're the foolest of fools, Philips.

And yes, I'm hyperaware 'foolest' isn't even a word, but let's just pretend it is.

I flicker my eyes open, ready to take the bus all the way home with my head hung low, when something stops me. I don't know why, but my breath halts in my throat at the dark Doc Martens somebody stepping off the bus is wearing. I haven't glanced up yet, but those shoes look awfully familiar.

Doc Martens…

Unlaced…

A stitched white broken love heart on the side of the left one…

I swear I've seen them before but where?

Where? Where? Where?

And when it finally hits me, I internally gasp.

The picture! They were in that picture last month.

Wait, that would mean… No, no, it couldn't be. It can't.

As my gaze flickers higher, at the person descending the bus right in front of me, I slow by their studded leather jacket. And the moment those familiar melancholic onyx eyes bore into mine, I forget how to breathe.

Holy sweet Jesus, it's him.

Him.

Elijah Diesel.

And he's even more beautiful in person.

My mouth gets all dry and my hands become so sweaty holding *Rolling Stone* magazine that it slips from my grip. I cringe as it slides across the sidewalk like it's on skates. And I don't know if the timing could be any worse, but just as it slows, Elijah unintentionally stomps his feet right on the magazine.

Oops.

Almost on instinct, he picks up the magazine, stares at the cover, and then his eyes slowly flicker to the gap of sidewalk between us until they meet my pink platform sneakers.

Ever so slowly, his gaze rakes up my body with a sexily clenched jaw, and I'm happy to confirm his eyes are really that dark. It feels like a lifetime passes the way he's checking out my long, lean legs, my short skirt, and cropped white shirt with little floral-patterned peaches, some midriff exposed.

He stays there for a little while, and the longer his hot stare lingers, the more my chest heaves. My breaths are rushed and all frantic-like. I feel my nipples harden in arousal, stabbing through my lacy bra and outlining my shirt.

He does this to me.

He does this *all* to me.

And when those dreamy dark onyx eyes finally meet my face, my knees buckle.

The bus moves off behind him with a hiss, and it feels like we're in a slow-motion movie with the way his dark hair softly blows in the wind, the ends so wavy.

Arching a brow, Elijah gestures toward the magazine he's holding. "I think you dropped something, *Peaches*," he calls out to me, and *dear God*, his voice…

It's the perfect combination of a sexy raspiness and a murmur, as if he can disguise himself in them both, ready to pounce at any minute now.

Striding up to me, he extends the magazine out to me. Our fingers brush when I take it from him, and sizzling electricity shoots down my arm.

Gosh, this guy is a dream.

It feels so weird seeing Elijah up close after spending the past month looking at his picture all alone in my bedroom. *This is so much better.* I can't get over his musky, sandalwood scent with a hint of tobacco. It's a scent I've never smelled so up close before, and instantly I wish I could smell it forever.

Wow. He's so tall and I'm even wearing platform sneakers. He's easily six-two, six-three.

Wait a minute, did he just call me "Peaches?"

I nervously smile, an obvious blush crawling up my cheeks. "Umm, thank you."

Elijah nods, his broody gaze flickering between my eyes and my plump lips, which I can't help but softly bite.

He stares for a second longer, and just as his hot breath hits my lip, he steps back and begins walking away with such a swagger that his leather jacket sways from side to side.

Despite my fingers continuing to fizzle, a hollowness takes over my body and I don't know why. This was it, my chance to tell him whatever, and I just blew it. *Ugh!*

Chewing my lower lip, I watch as Elijah keeps on walking in the opposite direction of the convenience store. He must have lit up a cigarette in the seconds he walked away because now clouds of thick white smoke lace the air around him every so often.

He smokes.

Mama always tells me how bad smoking is. That neither me nor my older sister, Maya, should ever touch a cigarette. For the past years, I've believed her, thought it was such a dirty thing, but knowing *he* smokes changes everything.

He doesn't make it seem dirty as he looks both ways before jogging across the street, Elijah

Diesel makes smoking look like it's heaven's cure to all the chaos here on earth. And perhaps it's that reason alone, (or the fact that I'm still astonished that he was right in front of me), but I do the unexpected.

Quickly stuffing the magazine in my schoolbag, I sling the backpack over my shoulder and wait for the lights before running across the Tribeca street.

Even though Elijah's several feet ahead of me, his studded leather jacket is still in view, and I use it as my guide while I weave through people, apologizing and jogging faster until I'm mere inches away.

The damn guy keeps on walking faster, and here I am treading along behind him, not even knowing what I'd say if he turns around. All I do know is that his scent makes me feel like home, and I could get used to the cigarette smoke hitting me from ahead.

"Hey, watch where you're going!" A lady pushing a stroller growls when I almost run into her as I turn a corner five feet behind Elijah.

I turn to her, mortified. "Oh my God, I'm so sorry, please forgive me, I'm just…"

She comes to a halt with a glare. "I don't care what you're '*just*' doing, be careful around corners!"

I feel bad right to my core, but she walks off with her stroller before I can say anything else.

Breathing out a strangled breath, I vow to forget it completely and focus on Elijah, but when I turn back around and there's no sign of him or any leather jacket, I begin to panic.

No. No. No.

I did not just lose him!

Where could he have gone?

He didn't cross the street again and there's no way he could have entered the cafés a little farther down unless he bolted, which is... highly unlikely.

Damn.

I glance around, frustrated with myself this too was all for nothing.

Stuff it, I'm going home.

Spinning on my heels, I'm adamant to call it a day when I unexpectedly slam into a solid chest and tumble back, almost losing my balance.

My schoolbag slips and falls to the ground with a thud.

What the hell...?

The second I crane my head up and glance at my victim, I'm pretty sure I'm about to piss my pants. It's Elijah, and unlike before, there's a deadly look in his steel-black-eyed stare.

"Are you following me?" Elijah growls ever so

wickedly, stepping forward until we're only inches apart. "Because if you are, it ain't gonna be good for you, *Peaches*, believe me."

He continues to stare me down, awaiting my response, all while my mouth dries up and I wish I could just disappear. It doesn't matter how badly I've had a crush on him, right now if looks could kill... I'd be gone. Long gone.

Jerk.

I don't like the soullessness in his death glare or the way he clenches his jaw when I part my lips before closing them. I don't know this guy. At all. Which is why I do the only logical thing in my head during this current moment...

I take one last glance at my dark, edgy sinner, and then bolt in the other direction.

I run all the way home, (and yes, through the Brooklyn Bridge too) like I'm some sort of freak. It takes me over an hour, and by the end of it, I'm slow walking like I just won a marathon.

Or just came last.

But I keep on going until I lock myself in my bedroom, panting. And it's only then, as my breaths finally begin to stabilize, that I realize I no longer have my schoolbag. In fact, I don't think I ran home with it at all. It slipped from my shoulder when I slammed into Elijah's chest, and I never picked it up.

Oh. My. God.

He's with it. He has it.

And the worst part of all? I have a keyring on it with all of my information in case of an emergency.

My *name.*

My *number.*

My *home address.*

It's all at his fingertips.

Groaning, I dive onto my bed and bury my face into my silk pillow.

Ohhh no!

I'm so screwed.

Elijah Diesel is going to kill me!

Chapter
TWO

Elijah

If Hurricane Blondie thinks this is where our story ends, she's dead wrong.

Hurricane Blondie—that's exactly what she was the way she stormed into my life and left just as fucking fast. I mean, come on, it's one thing to drop your magazine; it's another to act like a complete psycho and stalk somebody down the street. It's exactly what Hurricane Blondie did to me; except she couldn't take the heat when I confronted her about it.

I've never seen a girl so scared in my entire life.

I'm used to the alternative rock, a little seductive

goth, the kind of girls who wear fishnet stockings, quirky barrettes, and paint their nails the brightest neon colors. Those who don't give a shit. But Hurricane Blondie ain't like that at all.

I saw straight through her as fear laced her eyes after I asked if she was stalking me. Her emerald-green eyes widened so much, for a moment it was as if I was staring into a field of rolling green meadows, something you'd find in the South of France, with their bitter fucking excuse of sour grapes in exchange for the name champagne.

Fuck that shit. I'm not a champagne kind of guy. *I could never be.*

I like the taste of liquor wrapped on my tongue like I like sex. Rough. Toxic. An overdose.

There's nothing fucking gentle about me. I mean, even my full name (it's real, by the way) alludes to something destructive. So, I get the fear in *Peaches's* eyes (*yes, that's what I'm calling her now*). I get her running away. I even get her not wanting to know a fuck about me. But what I don't get is why she left her damn schoolbag literally by my damn feet.

She couldn't have not noticed that she left it, and the fact that she still goes to high school… makes me wish I hadn't stared at those long, toned lean legs for *that* long as she ran.

She's got to be seventeen, or no more than

eighteen, the perfect age to fuck up a life with peer pressure, tobacco, and narcotics.

Trust me, been there, fucking done that, although my personal hell began much younger.

And as I stare out at Manhattan through my loft's black steel casement windows hours later, her damn schoolbag shoved in the corner of the living room, (next to my lyric notebook, bass guitar, and rolled-up joints), I wonder if she—*Peaches*—has ever been involved in any of those three situations.

Peer pressure.

Tobacco.

Narcotics.

Hmmm.

She seems too smart of a girl to let people force her into situations she detests. And there's no way she's snorting coke in the bathroom at parties with the A+ paper literally hanging out of her schoolbag.

That only leaves one… *tobacco.*

I piece my eyes shut, letting the memories of her run through my fucked-up mind much longer than they should.

Nah, I don't see the narcotics either, not with those plump, candy-floss-colored lips that seemed so soft.

I wanted to sexily bite that lip down, all fucking primal, and discover if *Peaches* was the kind of girl to gasp or to moan.

But I'm not the kind of guy to kiss and tell.

In fact, I don't fucking tell at all.

My bandmates are a testament to that. I may as well be the coldest motherfucker in Manhattan. Some say I lack a heart; I say I wasn't ever born with one. So this *Peaches* girl, whoever she fucking is, better tread carefully because I'm not the kind of guy you fuck over and then expect I'll forgive.

I don't forgive.

I don't forget.

I fight. Hard. In the silence. Until I get what I want, and when I get it, I never want to let it go.

I treat my wants like black-winged butterflies with unique dots of yellow. Because although I have them trapped in my imaginary spray-painted brass vintage cage, I let them flutter free within the constraints.

And right now, all I want is *Peaches*.

I storm over to her schoolbag in my bedroom and flip over the keyring, all her information bringing a devilish smirk to my lips.

All I want is you, Rosalia Philips.

I wanna know every single thing about you.

Why you chose me. Why you didn't let me go. Why you keep on replaying in my head, like the lyrics of a sickly depressive melody disguised in the sweetest honeyed sin of voices. *Yours.*

And when I find you, Rosalia, you're going to

wish you never ran away from the monster some call Elijah Diesel, but I call *"me."*

It takes barely five hours since Rosalia ran away from me for me to lose my self-control. The darkened ominous Manhattan clouds coat in midnight as I store her number in my phone.

Rosalia.

I decide I like her name.

I decide she suits it well.

I also decide she's a completely oblivious idiot for all of the information she leaves so freely on her schoolbag.

Fuck emergencies. If she loses it, somebody could stalk her ass and murder her. I hate people, I really fucking do, but the thought of such beauty vanishing makes me sick to my stomach.

So that's the first thing I'm going to tell her—to take this damn keyring off. The second? Well, you'll just have to see, won't you?

I'm not the kind of guy who texts or calls. I prefer seeing somebody's goddamn face, but for her, I'll make an exception… *just this once.*

Pulling out my phone from the pocket of my distressed jeans, I begin typing away and hit send.

ELIJAH: Are you aware of what you left behind when you ran away from me?

I don't expect her response to come so suddenly.

ROSALIA: Maybe.

Just maybe?

ELIJAH: Do you want it back?

My phone buzzes in my grip.

ROSALIA: Maybe.

My brows furrow. The fuck?

ELIJAH: Is **maybe** all you're gonna say?

ROSALIA: Maybe.

Fucking *maybe* again.

I grind my teeth because I don't know if she straight up doesn't know what else to say, or she's intentionally doing this to piss me off beyond repair. Either way, I don't like it.

Oh, is this how you wanna play it, huh? 'Cause I can fucking play, baby.

ELIJAH: Make up your mind, **Peaches**, or else I'm gotta dump it.

Her response comes back in exactly three seconds, and finally it's more than just *maybe*.

ROSALIA: Yes, I want it, please.

Please?

I almost scoff to myself.

Part of me likes how she didn't even ask who this number belonged to, she just assumed.

ELIJAH: Why did you run?

Those fucking bubbles do their dance, and then all of a sudden disappear. She leaves me on read. *Fucking read.* And if it's one thing in life I don't take, it's that.

My thumbs viciously throw daggers into my screen with every tap.

ELIJAH: Fine, continue keeping quiet, I'll be at your house in twenty minutes with your schoolbag.

That sure wakes her up.

ROSALIA: Oh, umm, I would prefer if you didn't come here. Can we meet somewhere public? Like a park? I know it's late but... I think a park is better.

ELIJAH: No. I'm coming to you so this time you won't run from me.

I sense the panic in her reply.

ROSALIA: The park would be better, please, Elijah.

ELIJAH: Not happening, **Peaches**.

And then I lock my phone, ignoring the following texts lighting up my screen—all from her. Because if it's something Rosalia should know about me, it's that I always win.

Always.

Just like I did right now.

And you better get used to it, Peaches, 'cause you just started a fucking war inside my mind.

Chapter
THREE

Rosalia

I wish I never bought that damn *Rolling Stone* magazine earlier today.

This is all my fault.

As I glance over every fast car that passes, wondering which one will belong to Elijah, the light inside my chest dims. Truth is, my heart hasn't stopped beating in frantically wild pitter-patters ever since Elijah's text.

My entire body froze up at the unknown number, knowing exactly who it was even before I read it. Coldness rippled down my spine, the same one still present as I sit on the porch steps of my family's Brooklyn Heights brownstone.

He found me.

I can't stop nervously tracing the black wrought iron laced railing. My legs haven't stopped tingling from my madwoman run through New York to Brooklyn from earlier. My poor feet were already so blistered from ballet that the run made it even worse. I had to rest them in a salt bath the second I got home. Luckily, I was the only one home and didn't have to explain anything to my parents or my older sister about it or Elijah because *that* would have been awkward.

It's been twenty minutes since Elijah's last text, which means he's moments away.

If he sticks to his word, that is.

I didn't expect him to want to come to my house because as much as he intrigues me, it's too personal. And risky. But if there's anything I've learned about him in the past six hours, it's that he's persistent. Dominant.

It's why I've already dialed 911 and all I have to do is hit that tempting green circle. Can I really trust Elijah alone? I don't know. I mean, I don't know even *who this guy is*. Yes, he was in *Rolling Stone* magazine and that should mean he at least has some decency, but that doesn't mean he's *not* a serial killer. I mean, just look at Ted Bundy's tactics, *like, erm, helloooo!*

Okay, so maybe it isn't the whole stranger danger thing I'm freaking out about. I'm freaking out because my conservative parents are sound asleep inside. My father doesn't have a shift at the hospital tonight, but he's on call, and if there's an emergency and his pager goes off... yep, he's going to trip over me running down these stairs.

I'd probably be grounded for the entire summer, and who wants that? Certainly not me.

As I said, it's risky.

Too risky.

But I really need my schoolbag... *and I kinda want to see Elijah Diesel again.*

Wrapping my arms around my waist, I rock back and forth on the step, the slightly warm New York air doing nothing to calm me down. Even though it's the start of summer, the nights are still chilly, no matter how intense the dose of humidity is.

I wait.

And wait.

And wait some more, imagining which kind of car he'll pull up in front of my brownstone at almost one o'clock in the morning will be.

It may be all sleek and flashy like an Audi, or perhaps he'll show up in a vintage Mustang, a toothpick in his mouth and a smolder like it's some late '50s rock and roll film. All I know is that whatever he drives, I'm certain it's glossy and onyx, just like his eyes.

I've never done anything like this—waited outside with my house key between my pointer and middle finger, ready to attack, just in case. Although this is an elite area of Brooklyn with gorgeous historic homes and tree-lined streets, I'm still cautious. Of everybody. Including that rocker called Diesel who's now five minutes late.

Brooklyn's late-night buzz fills the air with rumbling cars and lively music in the distance.

I roll my eyes, wondering if he's been playing me all along and is actually not coming, but then I hear a deep rumble in the distance like the sweetest of rough purrs. The sound gets louder and louder until it's deafening, and a gasp escapes me when a Harley Davidson speeds up my street.

My eyes widen.

Could it be...?

Holy shit!

The Harley's roaring so loud, I'm pretty sure this guy just woke up the entire neighborhood, the five New York boroughs, *and* New Jersey!

The Harley, which is the sleekest one I've ever seen with a glossy onyx wrap and cool silver accents, comes to a slow right outside my brownstone.

The rider has a black helmet on, and the visor is down, preventing me from seeing anything under the warm glow of the art deco streetlight. But the moment my gaze moves to the spiky leather jacket, my heart jolts.

It's him.

He cuts the engine, kicks down the motorbike's kickstand, unclips his helmet, and hangs it on one of the handlebars in all less than three seconds. It tells me riding his Harley isn't just something he does, it's habitual. His livelihood. I'm sure he could ride the metal monster eyes closed.

When Elijah's hooded eyes finally meet mine, they darken, and all the air in my lungs is sucked out of me.

Oh my God.

Elijah doesn't drop his stare as he softly bites down on the tips of one of his tan leather gloves and winks before roughly yanking it off. He repeats the action with his other biker glove, and between that and his inky tattooed hands, it's the sexiest thing I've ever witnessed.

Too bad he could be a serial killer.

Elijah sets the gloves in his saddlebag and climbs off his Harley, raking a hand through his sexily tousled hair. Confidently striding up to me,

Elijah slips his hands into his jean pockets, and he looks like heartbreak. A pure bad boy with the midnight moon cascading down his body, the silvery moonlight illuminates all the things that speak to me the most.

His deep Cupid's bow leading to those sinful, kissable lips.

His small gold hoop earring in his left ear with a detailed skull and angel wings hanging. Silver rings that beam in the light.

His wavy dark hair, which is wet and now slicked back, giving me the impression he just showered before he came here. A few strands hang low, some covering his eyes, and it instantly reminds me of Depp's *Cry Baby*.

In this moment, I'm kind of glad I didn't rip that picture of him in my scrapbook into a million tiny little pieces when I ran home. I want to stare at him forever, without him knowing. But that all ends when Elijah flicks his eyes to me.

"Hi," is the first thing that escapes my lips.

Obviously, it's a bad choice with the way his jaw ticks and he looks away. He continues climbing the porch steps, beyond the step I'm sitting on.

Huh?

Melancholic Sin literally walks past me until he's standing by my front door, his back to me.

"Um, excuse me?" I clear my throat; well

aware I shouldn't get so lost in the lingering whiff of his musky sandalwood cologne. "Elijah, where are you going? I'm right here."

Elijah doesn't dare turn around, forcing me to stare at his broad shoulders and... I squint and twist my body around to see it better... *Is that F. Scott Fitzgerald's* The Beautiful and Damned *tucked in his back pocket?*

Yes, yes, it is, Rosalia.

How the heck did he ride here with that thing under his ass?

I'm confused because from just looking at Elijah, he doesn't seem like the kind of guy who would adore literature, especially the classics... *Because classics are what I like too.*

I wonder if he's read To Kill A Mockingbird, *the book I have safely tucked inside my school bag and constantly reread.*

And just like that, Elijah opens his mouth and ruins it all.

"I said I was coming *to your house*, not *to your porch*," he grumbles, like being here at one o'clock in the morning is the last place he wants to be. "You want your bag, I'm stepping in."

My jaw drops.

Is this guy serious?

I can just imagine my father coming down and seeing this eyeliner-wearing rocker with his seventeen-year-old daughter… Forget me being grounded for a summer, I'd be grounded for life.

"Well, no, you can't go inside." I laugh nervously because it's the only other thing I can do despite panicking. "So, you either give me my schoolbag here or I'll call the police for stolen property."

Glancing over his shoulder, Elijah eyes me for the longest time before scoffing. "Seriously? *Stolen property*? You're fucking lucky I brought the bag home with me to begin with."

"I *am* appreciative. Trust me, I am, but you can't come in. My parents are inside, and I…"

"You, *what*?"

"I'd prefer if we stayed out here."

Elijah gives me nothing as he shakes his head and faces the door with a shrug. "Well, I guess I'll just ring the doorbell then, won't I?"

Now it's my turn for the entire neighborhood, the five New York boroughs, *and* New Jersey to hear my shocked gasp. "You wouldn't…"

Elijah chuckles darkly.

"Oh, I totally would." He lingers his fingers inches from the glamorous oak and solid brass lion head doorbell. "Try me, *Peaches*. I'll press it so goddamn hard, you'll wish you just opened the door to begin wi—"

Standing up, I cut him off. "Would you please stop with all your ultimatums?"

"The world doesn't care for a *please*. I sure don't."

Ahhh!!!

I huff and give in, mounting the steps until I'm right beside him. It's there where I narrow my eyes, making sure he sees my deep, cruel glare. "You know, for a guy who was in *Rolling Stone* magazine, you act just like every other guy."

"Oh, how's that?"

"An asshole."

Elijah slowly smirks, and I hate that I find myself drooling. "*Oh*, you saw my article, did you? So you're not only a stalker, but you're also an ultra-stalker. I assume you were reading that new *Rolling Stone* magazine today to see if I was in that edition too, huh?"

Mind reader.

"No, not at all." Shaking my head, I jab my house key into the keyhole. "I have better things than staring at you all day, believe me."

You're such a liar, Rosalia Philips.

"Good. Now, do you want your damn bag or not?"

"Yes," I grit through my teeth, just as my front door clicks unlocked. I hold the knob close, keeping the door ajar.

Within seconds, Elijah's jogging down the porch steps and then back up again with my schoolbag. He had it in the big saddlebag at the back of his Harley.

When he's beside me again and I go to cheekily grab it from him, he slings it over his shoulder and glares down at me in his six-foot-three frame. "Nice try. As I said, I ain't afraid to buzz that doorbell, *Peaches*, so quit the good girl act."

"It isn't an act," I whisper and slowly step into my house with a finger pressed against my lips to signal silence. "Follow me, don't speak, and if it's anything you do, don't make a sound."

Elijah flicks his gaze beyond me, toward the house. "It's dark in there. I can't see shit."

I shoot him a death glare. "Well, you better figure it out, *amigo*, or else I'll kick you."

"Mmhmmm." Giving me a once-over, a smoldering smirk breaks out on his lips. "I'd like to see you try…"

I get lost in those eyes that swirl challenge.

I don't give in to him, no matter how badly I can feel my heartbeat lodged in my throat from how close we're standing.

When I finally look away, I suck in a breath and step to the side, so that Elijah can step in. His leather jacket brushes against my bare arm, like scorching fire attempting to unintentionally light me up. I let it go.

In the dark, Elijah follows me through my brownstone and up the two flights of stairs, until we're on the third level of my brownstone. I cringe at my parents' soft snores from the opposite side of the hall, highly aware there's an older man walking right behind me. Thank God my older sister is staying at her boyfriend's tonight because I swear that girl is nocturnal.

My plan sinks before I can victory dance when my bare foot hits that damn dodgy spot on the oak hardwood floor just outside my bedroom. It squeaks—*loudly.*

Oh no.

I freeze, but Elijah couldn't have known and blindly slams into me hard from behind with a big *oof.* Before I know it, we're stumbling forward, and I have just enough time to cover my face, bracing for impact.

Hands sink into my hips, slightly easing the velocity as I slam into my bedroom door, my face receiving the brunt of it.

Bang. Bang. Bang.

Oh shit.

Oh shit.

Oh shit.

Elijah stumbles with me, his body crashing

into mine from behind, pressing up against the door. A low groan escapes his throat, and the warm breath tickles my neck, taunting me. My ass digs into him, and I don't know if I want to disappear or burst out laughing.

"What happened to making no noise?" Elijah whispers in my ear, the taunting smirk evident in his sexily raspy voice.

I thank God we're in the dark because I swear my cheeks are burning.

"Shut up. I think I just rearranged my face," I groan.

"You okay?"

Oh my God, is Mr. Mysterious concerned for me?

"I will be."

But my words mean nothing when I hear rustling from my parents' bedroom.

My father's snores have stopped.

Yikes!

Opening my bedroom door, I quickly shove Elijah inside and softly shut the door in his face, just as my father opens his bedroom door. The hall light flickers on, blinding me like I'm some type of vampire that hasn't seen the outside world for six long centuries.

My father narrows his gaze at me, shielding

his eyes to look at me better. "Rosalia, everything okay?"

My heart is beating like crazy, knowing one slip-up could ruin this entire plan.

Yes, Dad, I'm okay, just have a Harley lover hiding in my bedroom, but it's all good, he's into Fitzgerald.

"Yeah, sorry." I smile. "I just went down to get some water and tripped up the stairs. I'm okay now."

"You sure? That sound woke me up." Concern is written all over his face. "Does anything hurt?"

I giggle, knowing his doctor side would come out. "I'm completely fine, Dad, I promise. I just got a fright, that's all."

My father goes to speak, but a yawn comes out instead. He chuckles, his light eyes warming as he nods toward his bedroom. "All right, if you say so, sweetheart. I'm heading back to bed. Good night."

I lean against my bedroom door as he flicks off the light. "Night, night."

I wait until my father's door shuts and then what feels like three minutes later until his soft snores fill the hall. When I step into the darkness that is the bedroom and blindly lock my door, I shut my eyes, wanting to kick myself for letting this go this far.

There's a grown man somewhere in my room.

A damn grown man who was in *Rolling Stone* magazine.

The same man I became obsessed with in less than a month, adamant to know everything about him, and look where it got me—frantically rushing around my room like a madwoman.

I can't remember where I placed my candles because turning on the wall sconce lights at a time like this would be deadly with Elijah in here.

What if my dad wakes up again and sees the bright glow beneath my door?

What if he sees Elijah's shadow?

Hears his voice?

Nooope, the candles are far safer. Softer.

Only... *where the heck did I put them?*

Blindly reaching for my curtains, I pull them all the way up and let the soft silvery moonlight drown my bedroom. I almost jump when I see where Elijah is. He's sitting on the corner of my bed, simply waiting for me with a less than impressed glare.

My schoolbag is on the floor, on the edge of the bed. Home sweet home.

Maybe I don't need those candles after all...

"Soooo," I whisper, consciously wrapping my arms over my petite waist. "You're in my house, I have my schoolbag. This sneak upstairs was all for nothing, really. *Now* can you go?"

Completely ignoring me, Elijah's eyes drop to my chest and my body reacts. Heat rushes across my veins because I've never been looked at like this before. He looks at me as if I'm more than just Rosalia Philips—the organized, introverted, Brooklyn ballerina. He looks at me like I'm human. Like I'm worth something.

Glancing down, I subtly eye my tits and how obvious my hard nipples are outlined, even through my lacy pink bra. I know I should be ashamed of it, but for some outlandish reason, I'm not.

Elijah Diesel's a dark, twisted fantasy, the kind good girls like me shouldn't ever imagine.

I wonder what he would feel like. What hugging him would do to me. Wonder if I let him kiss me, if he'd recklessly use his tongue to devour me, and if he'd taste like musky tobacco or more like a fresh peppermint.

Eyes still on me, Elijah whispers in the low light, "How old are you, Rosalia?"

"Seventeen," I murmur back, rubbing my thumbs over the thin fabric of my top. "How old are you?"

"How old am I?"

"Mmhmmm."

"Why do you ask?"

I shrug.

"No, tell me…" He stands. "Why do you ask?"

"Conversation starter?" I say, but it comes out as more of a question if anything. *Darn me.*

Elijah clenches his cleanly shaven jaw. "I ain't trying to start a damn conversation, *Peaches.*"

Okay, idiot, maybe I should have read your Rolling Stone *article after all. If I did, I would have known how much of a cold-hearted asshole you were in two-point-five seconds and would have never followed you.*

I get all worked up and actually start to hate him.

"You're in my bedroom at one o'clock in the morning. I think *you* owe *me* a *conversation.*"

"All right, I'll give you something. Take that keyring off your bag. The one with all your information. You don't know the number of freaks you could attract with it on there."

"*Oh,*" I scoff, the next words escaping before I can help it. "You mean *freaks* like *you*?"

My jaw instantly drops.

Oh.

My.

God.

I did not just say that.

I hate myself for it because I don't think he's a freak, *at all.* I was just angry, that's all.

Darkness takes over his eyes that I can only describe as completely emotionless. Pure carnage.

"Oh God." I slap a hand over my mouth with wide eyes. "I'm so sorry, I didn't mean t—"

"The fuck you didn't," Elijah growls through the skin of his teeth, probably doing his best to talk low, but I can hear the anger bubbling through. "If I'm just a fucking freak to you, then good, I guess in the end it's better this way."

"Elijah, please, I didn't mean it. I was just angry and—"

"Good night, *Peaches.*"

And then without another word, Elijah storms out of my bedroom door, leaving golf-ball-sized guilt lodged in my throat.

I stand here, in the middle of my bedroom, lost.

I feel so bad.

I didn't mean to anger him. I just said those things in the heat of the moment. What hurts me the most was the glimmer of sadness that pooled in Elijah's eyes seconds before he left.

It kills me.

It was as if I had shot a silver bullet right into his chest, and that tough armor surrounding him began to fade away, stripping bare the real person Elijah Diesel truly is—a real sad boy.

The roar of his Harley has me rushing to turn

around and glance outside my window, just making it in time as my gorgeous villain pulls out of my tree-lined street. And as he rides away, every echo of his metal beast ricochets into my sad heart.

It's only after I collapse on my bed with a frown that I realize something's digging into my pajama-covered thigh. I glance down, noticing the perfectly blue-bound classic book.

The Beautiful and Damned.

It's so ironically us, only there isn't an *us*. But if there were, I'd be the damned. After all, it's a story of tragedy, nonetheless. It must be.

I gasp because this is Elijah's book. *Elijah's.* It must have slipped from his pocket when he stood.

I caress the pad of my finger over the title, outlining it, wondering if I'll ever see him again. My vision turns glassy at the thought that I won't.

I continue to hate myself for tearing up over the guy. The guy who stole my breath since the first moment I saw him, and who even though is upfront and a little rude, had just enough kindness in his heart to bring me back my schoolbag.

Flicking through the first pages of the heavy book, I gasp when I see it's a first edition. I almost don't want to touch it anymore; too afraid I'll ruin it somehow. I'm just about to close it when I notice a message written on the title page in a thick black marker… and it confirms everything.

Oh my God.

My throat throbs, aching. I didn't expect this at all because I just ruined everything.

He wrote a personalized note… to me.

Peaches,

I saw in your backpack that you enjoy the classics, so I thought I should give you another.

Keep it, it's yours now.

I've reread it a million times.

Call me when you finish it, or whatever,

—E

Elijah Diesel didn't accidentally leave this F. Scott Fitzgerald bittersweet classic on my bed. He left it on purpose.

For me.

And that's when the first hot tear slips.

Chapter
FOUR

Rosalia

I read *The Beautiful and Damned* in an entire sitting the next day.

Tragic. Bittersweet. Beautiful. A literary classic wrapped in a dream. And by the end, (well, even before the end), I so desperately wanted to tell him everything and anything about it.

I hesitated.

And hesitated more.

Then, I finally called Elijah.

The first call rang once, then it was obvious he ended it.

The second rang out for a damn century until I reached his voice mail.

The third rang straight to his voice mail; meaning he had switched off his phone.

None of this is his fault. I keep on trying to tell myself that.

It's *my* fault I was stupid enough to follow him around Tribeca.

It's *my* fault I let anger overrule and called him a freak when he's far from that.

It's *my* fault I was crazy enough to call him, even though he had written that note before coming to my house, then later stormed out.

Now, it's been two months without Elijah, and I don't know what to do to fix it. I'm not saying we have to be best friends; I'm not saying we even have to see each other again if he really doesn't want to, all I want to do is apologize.

I hate fighting.

This is slowly becoming the worst summer of my life because I'm so tempted to search him up, but I don't want to. I want to know him for *him* through *him*.

I know he's probably some hotshot. I mean, if he's in *Rolling Stone* magazine, he kind of has to be, right? But there must be so much more to him than a single Google search can uncover, especially the person he is.

All I know is that I hate this.

I want to go back to before I made a fool out of myself.

You're not a freak, Elijah Diesel. I wish you could just believe me.

When I think of a perfect life, I can't see myself in it. I don't know why. I just think there are parts of me that are so disconnected from this wicked thing we call life, that at times I feel so numb.

I have good parents now.

I live on a good side of the city.

I have good grades, good friends, a good heart.

It's summer, for damn's sake, and yet I feel like my entire world is crumbling from the inside out.

Truth is, ever since I stumbled across Elijah months ago in that magazine, I've felt... different. No, I've *wanted* to feel different. I'm sick of the same old mundane life I've been conditioned to live. There's no thrill. No joy. It's the same thing on repeat, every single day.

I'm sure Elijah's life isn't like this.

There must be a little thrill in his.

Thrill.

Risk.

Challenge.

All those things excite me and have passion bubbling at the pit of my stomach.

I want to do something adventurous before this summer is over. *Even just one.* One thing that doesn't include my usual good girl act. I want to… I don't know. Trespass. Go to a party. Take one puff of a cigarette. Anything that makes me feel more alive.

I crave that adrenaline, the nervousness of getting caught, the palpitations in your chest you get before doing something crazy—like skydiving (which I'm going off second-degree excitement because I've never done it, but my best friend has).

Second-degree excitement? Goddddd, that's so depressing.

Why can't I be that girl who jumps out of an airplane at fourteen-thousand feet? *Because with your luck, Rosalia Philips, you'll be the exception and somehow tumble to your death.*

I feel sick just thinking about it, but I've been playing life comfortable for too long. I want something more, and fortunately (or unfortunately), I know just where to find it.

Cue Naomi Ryder—my best friend, and the only person in the world who truly knows me inside out. Naomi and I have been best friends since we were six, when I stepped into ballet class for the very first time. We've been at each other's hips ever since. Through all the ups and downs. I love her to pieces.

She once fell in love with an English exchange student with a crazy soccer-style mid-fade. On their fifth date (*and yes, Naomi was counting*), he confessed that he was gay and only told her now because he felt bad and just went along with it.

Yup. For realsies, peeps. That happened.

It was safe to say that freshman year with him, her, and me in basically all the same classes was realllllly interesting. She was so broken-hearted for two weeks straight that I forced her (well, she was a willing participant) to watch (re-watch on my behalf) all of Matt Bomer's films with me, just so she could feel my pain that—he too—was gay.

Why are gay guys always the most beautiful?

Side note: She forgot about Brit boy *real* fast and grew an obsession with Matty B instead.

I let it go, but at the same time, fourteen-year-old me in my head said, *Um, rudeee, he's mine, thanks.* But Naomi's my best friend, and if this whole thing had to be a trio, so be it.

And as Naomi paces up and down my bedroom now, blabbing on about this cool restaurant that just opened up, I sink into my bed more with a frown.

I wish I were as gorgeous as her. She has the most perfectly silk brunette hair, always with those bouncy curls that are—wait for it—natural. If I wanted to get those curls, it'll take me over an hour and my mom is a HAIRDRESSER.

Brunette hair and piercing blue eyes, it's the rarest combination in my opinion, and yet Naomi is the exception. She's beautiful, beyond skin deep. I think Naomi is one of the kindest people alive, always with a pep in her step, *buttt* also has a little wild side within her that tonight I really need to feed off.

As I said, I want to do something a little crazy at least once this summer, and Naomi is my gal.

"Babe." She sighs, snapping her fingers in my face as she blindly coats her lips with even more gloss. "Are you even listening to me?"

I clear my throat. Oops.

"Yeah," I lie, rocking back and forth on my bed. "You were, like, talking about that wild restaurant that opened up downtown, right?"

Naomi doesn't seem the slightest bit amused. She's still depressed because her annual family vacation to France over the summer was canceled because her parents thought a getaway with just the two of them would be a great 'honeymoon revival.'

But it isn't all bad. She gets to spend the rest of the summer with me. Oh yes, that's right, this next month is going to be fun, and I'm not going to think of Elijah—at all.

Yeah, let's see how long that lasts.

But the whole Naomi-staying-over thing is rather fitting, really, seeing as my older sister, Maya, moved out only last week to Los Angeles for college. Naomi took over her room. I'm going to miss Maya a heck of a lot, but I think the number of times I've scarred myself tripping over one too many of her moving boxes in our hallway during the past week has made up for it.

"Yoooo, girl, are you tripping?" Naomi laughs, breaking me out of my haze for the second time tonight. It's only after she waves a hand in front of my face that a slow, mischievous smirk works up her lips. "Or are you really just thinking about him?"

"About whom?"

She gives me a 'no shit' look. "*Him.*"

I knew exactly who she meant from the start.

Elijah Diesel.

And it's precisely in this second that I half regret telling Naomi about Elijah, namely because she hasn't stopped teasing me about it, and second, she thinks he's a psychopath, (which he's not).

I laugh. *Laugh.* "No, not at all. I've already forgotten about him. I mean, who gives somebody a first edition and never answers their calls?"

"You called him a freak for a reason, Rosalia, because he *is* one."

There's a pang in my chest as my laughter flattens. "No, he isn't... Can you not remind me about that?"

"I'm sorry, but I just want to remind you that he doesn't deserve even thinking about. Besides, if he really was thinking about you too, he would have answered."

She isn't wrong regarding the calls. I mean, he really must hate me if he never called back.

"I know but... I can't stop thinking this is all my fault."

Softly smiling, Naomi sits on the bed beside me. "Babe, it isn't. This isn't on you."

I get all nervous, playing with my hands. "Then why do I feel like it is?"

Silence laces the space between us, and I hate it. I hate everything about this.

"You know what you need..." Naomi says after a little while.

I already know it's a bad idea the second her baby blue eyes sparkle. "Oh no, no, Naomi."

"You need a *distraction*!"

"No, I don't." I almost laugh. "The last time you said that, I had a damn vibrator arrive the next day."

Naomi wiggles her brows. "Well, hey, a vibrator is better than some seventeen-year-old heartbreak shit, but in saying that, I think this time you really need somebody to fuck all the anger out. Like, I don't know, a one-night stand or something."

My jaw drops.

Umm... what did she just say?

I look at her as if she's crazy. "And get emotional attachment issues for the rest of my life? Yeah, no, thanks, I'd rather die a virgin."

"Nooooo, Rosa, don't say that!" Naomi dramatically groans, falling on my bed and looking up at me as if I'm some heavenly angel. "It doesn't have to come with any emotional attachment. You just need to let go. That's all it is. The feeling... it's so *euphoric* and *real*. There's nothing like it, believe me."

Thump.

Thump.

Thump.

That's my heart, peeps, slowly going into overdrive.

I sigh because I get what my best friend is saying, I really do, but there's no way in hell I'll go there with a random stranger. I want my first time to mean something, not just throw it away to forget about another guy who probably doesn't even remember my name.

And then comes that damn devil on my shoulder that taunts me in ways it shouldn't…

Maybe Naomi is right. Maybe that crazy, wild thing you do this summer is break your forever dry spell, Rosalia Philips. Nowadays, everybody your age has already had sex anyway, including Naomi.

The smirk doesn't leave her lips. "Just think about it, Rosalia, okay?"

I nod with a small smile, even though I know I won't.

"Oh my God!" Naomi suddenly grins, standing up from my bed so fast, she has to readjust her short silver metallic dress after accidentally flashing me her tits. "I know what we can do tonight!"

"*Tonight*?" I screech, glancing over at my alarm clock. "Girl, it's ten thirty. The night's over."

Naomi dramatically groans. "Ugh! You're my best friend. You shouldn't be this introverted!"

"Sorry, not sorry." I grin with a wink.

"Besides, aren't you tired? I am. We literally had intense ballet practice all day until six."

"Ballet ain't gonna stop me from partying my little heart out. Noah's party literally just started! We can get there in say… an hour? It'll be great for both of us. Come on, Rosalia! You know I'm really into Noah and if I play my cards right, something can happen before senior year begins in less than two weeks. Besides, think of all your hot options there!"

I glance down at what I'm wearing. Oh yeah, that's right—*my pajamas*—just like A NORMAL HUMAN WOULD BE WEARING after ten o'clock on a *Tuesday* night.

Ugh!

"Fine." I playfully roll my eyes but end up laughing when Naomi literally jumps on top of me on the bed and rolls us around in a hug.

"Oh my God! I love you! I love you! I love you!"

And then the real night begins. We spend the next half hour cross-legged on my bedroom floor, doing our hair and putting on makeup in front of my mirrored wardrobe doors.

This week my father's away on a medical conference in Seattle and took my mom with him, so I don't have to worry about coming up with an excuse for them. It's not that they don't trust me.

They just don't trust the people at these parties and the possibility of me being exposed to liquor, drugs, or sex—*or all three.*

Drugs… a trigger.

It's just after eleven when best friend privileges begin to roll out. Naomi does my waterline, I do hers, she tells me I did a shit job, so I do it again. I tell her I literally have nothing to wear, and she sorts through my closet and pulls out a cherry-red satin crop top with thin lace straps and a real short denim pleated skirt for me to wear.

I don't even remember those being in my closet.

Naomi runs out of my room to the guest/her bedroom, and when she returns, she flings me a pair of her red stilettos.

"Don't wear a bra," she tells me, fluffing up her hair in the mirror. "Your huge tits will steal the show in that silk number."

"I don't know about *huge…*"

Naomi meets my gaze in the mirror and smirks. "Shut up, bitch, don't make me jealous. You're the greatest exception to ballet with those tits and are part of the zero-point-two percent that are going to make it in the industry based on your immense talent. You and I both know they're huge. Gah, it's honestly so unfair because you're so petite. Your modesty annoys me."

I snicker and get naked in front of her. Once I'm dressed, I walk over to my dresser and pull out a thin lacy white choker I bought weeks ago but haven't worn yet.

I run my finger over the detailed grooves of the lace, unsure as to why my breaths become labored over the fact the choker reminds me of Elijah. It's just something I can really see him liking on a girl.

I slip it on.

Light emerald eyes stare back at me when I glance at myself in my mirrored wardrobe. Naomi bumps her hip to mine. I smile, actually looking… decent. *Whoa.* The beach waves of my honey blonde hair make the fiery red of my soft eye-shadow, crop top, and stilettos really pop. I rub a glossy nude lipstick on my lips, and I'm done.

If it were up to me, I would have rocked up in a K.I.S.S. tee, jeans, and my hair in the messy bun it previously was. Aside from being such an introvert, it's why I never go out to parties without Naomi by my side.

I'm honestly her mom, *literally.*

Naomi does the drinking. I do the driving.

Naomi grinds on the hottest jocks at our high school. I daydream while sitting on a sticky couch with a full-on porno happening beside me.

Naomi glares down Noah Jacobs's girlfriend. I apologize to his girlfriend with a nervous smile because I'm pretty sure she could punch me in the face.

The same thing happens every single time, and to tell you the truth, I wouldn't want it any other way.

Just before I leave my bedroom behind Naomi, I glance over my shoulder and my gaze flickers to something catching my eye on the nightstand.

The Beautiful and Damned first edition.

The one *he* gave me.

Peaches,

I saw in your backpack that you enjoy the classics, so I thought I should give you another.

Keep it, it's yours now.

I've reread it a million times.

Call me when you finish it, or whatever,

—E

Gosh.

Sucking in a sharp breath, I flicker my bedroom light off and walk out the door without ever looking back.

Chapter
FIVE

Rosalia

The drive to Noah's penthouse in Manhattan is filled with off-key singing and talking about what we want to do before the end of August/summer in less than two weeks. So far Naomi has five million things on her list, and I have zero.

When we finally get there at eleven thirty, I manage to park my vintage mint green Fiat 500 around the corner, and we're walking to Noah's place with our arms looped in record time.

The tinge of humidity in the air outside is instantly demolished by the cooling inside Noah's lush penthouse apartment (well, his parents' anyway).

Even though I've been here before, it seems so much bigger than last time.

Marble.

Marble.

Marble.

It's all I see.

Oh, and gazillion familiar faces of us upcoming twelfth-grade seniors.

The blasting doof-doof music and sweaty bodies grinding all up together give me major claustrophobia. *Seriously.* My throat starts to close up and I don't know where to move without accidentally bumping into some jock and them getting the wrong idea.

Part of me silently wishes I had just stayed in the comfort of my home, but then I remind myself of what I said earlier—that nothing good comes out of playing life too comfortable—so here I am at a high school party at almost midnight, but I'm here with Naomi, so that makes it better.

Naomi launches for the red Solo cups and downs the illegal liquor, then cheers at the top of her lungs when a group of three jocks swarms us. I, like always, don't let a drop of liquor fall on my tongue, and instead keep an eye on Naomi and the jocks, ensuring they don't get too handsy with her.

"Rosalia Philips," one of them I recognize as Cayden, the star quarterback, smirks, and not so subtly eyes my tits. "Fuck, you look so hot, baby. I didn't know you'd be here tonight."

I almost want to roll my eyes into the back of my head.

First, I'm not your baby.

Second, your tongue was practically down the cheer captain's throat a mere second ago. So, thanks, but no, thanks.

"Hi, Cayden." I softly smile, still trying to be respectful. "Yeah, it was a last-minute kind of thing. Naomi really wanted to come, and I guess it was a good idea for me to get out of the house, you know."

Cayden's smirk deepens as he hooks an arm around my waist and pulls me close.

His warm lips brush over my ear, so it's his voice I can hear above the music when he whispers, "Well, if you want to *get out of the house* more often and put that gorgeous mouth of yours to good use, all you've got to do is ask." He pulls away to glance between my eyes slowly. "Yeah?"

I cringe. *Actually* cringe.

"No, thanks. I, umm… I have a boyfriend."

Arching a brow, Cayden's smirk crumbles. "You have a boyfriend?"

I clear my throat and wish my voice didn't come out as squeaky as it does when I say, "Yeah, I do. Just ask Naomi."

When his head snaps my best friend's way, I curse. *I didn't think he ACTUALLY would.*

"Yo, Naomi, baby! Does your girl over here have a boyfriend?"

Naomi, who was giggling at something one of the two jocks beside her said seconds ago, snaps her attention to Cayden.

Her brows furrow. "You talking to me?"

"Yeah. Does Rosalia have a boyfriend or not? 'Cause she said she did, but I've never seen the guy."

Her baby blue gaze snaps to mine.

My eyes widen and I subtly nod. *Yes, say yes.*

Naomi turns back to Cayden with a Cheshire grin. "Oh yeah, she has a boyfriend, all right."

Ahhh, sweet relief.

As my breaths stabilize, I promise myself I'll love Naomi forever for saving my ass.

"From school? How come I never see him?"

Naomi casually shrugs. "Dunno why you don't see him, but he always picks her up. He's older, like fifteen years older, got a band and everything. A real hottie. Isn't that right, Rosa?"

You know what I said about my breaths five seconds ago? About them *stabilizing*? Yeah, forget I ever said it because the opposite happens.

Nerves ripple through my blood with every heavy thump in my chest.

Oh my God!

Did Naomi just reference who I think she just referenced?

In the same moment, their four heads snap my way. The glare in Cayden's eyes is deadly as I think on the spot.

Crap. Crap. Crap.

I can't even widen my eyes because they'll notice. What do I say?

Naomi wiggles her brows with a smirk, and I want to strangle her for teasing me like this.

"Yeah," I lie with the most genuine fake smile I can manage. "He's really into rock and roll."

And thereeee goes Cayden, roughly slamming his shoulder into me as he storms off into the partying crowd.

Naomi throws me a playful wink as she returns to talking to the two jocks. Well, not before I made her be witness to my pointer finger, which I use as a fake knife to slice across my throat.

Naomi - 1.

Rosalia - 0.

It feels like we've been at this party for five years, but as I glance at my phone, it's only been two hours. *Two.* One thirty a.m. brightly stares back at me, taunting me for all the times I *wished* my parents would allow me to stay up this late.

As I sink farther into Noah's leather couch, observing sixteen and seventeen-year-olds going crazy all around with girls leaned back with their mouths wide, giggling as guys pour vodka into their mouths and their friends shout, "*swallow, swallow, swallow*," I wonder when exactly in my life I didn't get the memo.

The memo to be like them.

Free. Carefree. Without fear.

I wish I could be like them. Like Naomi. But I have a fear that nothing lasts forever, and it fucks me over, even when I try to escape it. I have my reasons to believe every single person in my life will one day disappear and abandon me, so I've tightened my circle so much so that when that day does come, the hurt will only come in four.

My father.

My mother.

My sister, Maya.

Naomi.

Nobody else can leave me because nobody else but those four people matter to me.

But as I eye Naomi dancing on the impromptu dance floor in the middle of the living room, slowly inching closer to Noah, who's laughing with his girlfriend, I wonder if that floating fifth person will fade before he ever was permanent.

Naomi—who for some reason isn't going as hard on the drinks tonight—waves me over to join her with a girly smile. But I've danced with her for the past two hours, and if I dance any more, I'm certain I'll be out of ballet tomorrow and that definitely won't be a good thing.

I signal I'll be there soon, and she playfully flips me off before she continues dancing.

Smiling, I glance back down at my phone, my blonde waves covering my eyes. There isn't a real-life porno happening beside me on the couch tonight (well, early morning), but there is a breakup, and suddenly I don't know what's worse.

The poor redhead I swear I had chemistry with last year can't stop sobbing, and it's those sobs that are the soundtrack to my mindless scrolling through my phone.

What to do…

The devil has me pressing on my messages, but it's my own curiosity that has me scrolling down to Elijah's name.

It's been over two months to the day since we last texted, or should I say since he told me he was coming to my house at midnight to return my schoolbag and I told him I'd prefer to meet somewhere else, and he just ignored the rest of my texts.

I'm so tempted to text Elijah.

To try one final time.

He ignored all my calls after I finished the F. Scott Fitzgerald classic, but he's got his text read receipts on, so I'll be able to see if he *intentionally* ignores my messages too and leaves me on read.

I know better than to message people at this hour, but seeing as he messaged me close to midnight the last time, I break all rules of common decency.

I bite my lower lip, drowning out the rumbling noise around and type away.

Should I really send it?

My thumb hovers over 'send.'

Stuff it.

I hit send.

Done.

> Rosalia: If you don't reply to this, I'm deleting your number.

I don't expect 'delivered' to flicker to 'read' so fast, or for my heart to slow when it does.

> Elijah: Don't.

Don't?

I haven't spoken to him in two months, and this is the first thing he says—*Don't.*

Ugh.

I blow out a sigh of frustration. The hell with this guy!

> Rosalia: Then tell me where I can meet you because I refuse to play this game any longer. We need to talk, Elijah. I think we both owe each other an explanation. When can I see you?

> Elijah: You can't. Besides, you should be asleep. It's almost two in the morning.

I snort and tap the little camera icon in the chat. Flipping it around so I see my face, I angle my phone high and take a sultry selfie of what I'm wearing. I make sure to cross my legs and cut the picture halfway across my face, so he can only see my glossy bit lip.

I've never been one to play it sexy—intentionally, anyway—but Elijah needs the push. He's not some seventeen-year-old you can just bat your lashes at. Elijah's much more.

He's a man.

An extremely complicated, broody alpha male.

But a man nonetheless… one very much older than me.

So strangely enough, I have a feeling the picture I just sent him of me on the couch with an eyeful of cleavage spilled and my skirt barely covering my panties will do just that—push him a little.

> Rosalia: Does this look like I'm sleeping to you? When can we meet? Elijah… ***Please***.

It takes Elijah exactly three minutes to reply, despite him seeing the photo the second I sent it.

> Elijah: Fuckkkk, don't send me things like that. Where are you? I'll pick you up.

I smirk.

Checkmate.

> Rosalia: You're not picking me up after avoiding me for TWO months. Tell me where to meet you. I'll take a taxi so I can leave my best friend my car.

> Elijah: You ain't going in a fucking taxi wearing *that*. Tell me where you are, ***Peaches***.

Peaches.

My heart shouldn't swell this much, but I can't help it. Swallowing thickly, I cast a glance in Naomi's direction as she grinds her ass against Noah, his girlfriend nowhere in sight.

Well, it looks like somebody got what they came here for.

I turn back to my phone.

After sending Elijah the address, he tells me he isn't far and will be here in five.

Five minutes.

I disappear into the hall and after finding a

bathroom that people aren't fucking each other in, go to the toilet and wash my hands. Warm emerald eyes stare back at me in the mirror as I push the strap of my purse farther up my shoulder.

The ball is in my court.

Elijah's going by my rules.

There's nothing to stress out about.

Except there is when I return to the living room. The first thing Naomi says when I hand her my Fiat's keys and tell her that I'm meeting up with Elijah is, "No, no, no, he could murder you, Rosalia! Please don't go out with him!"

Some teens around us snap their heads our way, but I'm just glad Cayden isn't within earshot.

Softly smiling at her concern, I reassuringly squeeze her shoulders. "He gave me a first edition. He's not going to murder me. I promise I'll be okay, okay? I'm just stressed about you driving home…"

"Don't be stressed. I literally only had one shot, but I'm worried about *you*…" Naomi slowly says, the light in her eyes dimming. "Are you sure this Elijah can be trusted? You didn't search him up, but I sure did. He's thirty-one Rosalia, *thirty-one* And guess what? He's going to be thirty-two this year! That's fifteen years older than us. Do you know how crazy that age gap is? And yes, he's in this upcoming alternative rock band, which okay, yes, it's pretty fucking cool, but *still*… I just love you, Rosa."

"I love you too, babe." I frown as I pull her into a tight embrace, her body sweaty from all the dancing, but I don't care. "I wouldn't be seeing him if I didn't trust him. Believe me, okay?"

Naomi sadly glances between my eyes until she finally gives in with a nod. "At least make me come out with you and see him, okay?"

I pull her into another embrace, my rosy scent merging with her patchouli one. "Okay."

We're out of Noah's penthouse in no time, glancing around for his sleek Harley, except there isn't one. Instead, double parked in front of a BMW is a glossy black vintage Chevrolet Camaro (I want to say late '60s) that screams his name. And scream his name it does as Elijah steps out of the driver's seat and… *whoa.*

He looks different. *So different.* A good different.

He has dark stubble, and it makes him look sexier than ever.

His alluring gaze is darker, harder, like a real standoffish rock star.

And, perhaps the most shocking, there's no sign of his signature leather jacket. Instead, he wears a white T-shirt that hugs his broad chest and taut torso. It exposes his beautiful light olive skin, those big muscular biceps, and inky black tattoos that cascade across each arm.

Elijah's gray-eyed stare pierces straight through

me, and electricity is all I feel light up my body. Sparks zoom across every inch of me at a million miles per hour.

He actually came.

But no matter how hard I want to smile; I keep my expression motionless.

"Holy shit, he's hot!" Naomi gasps under her breath, and before I know it, she's storming toward him in her five-inch heels.

"Hey! Asshole!" she grits, getting all up in his face, but he's so much taller that it's really in his chest. "I'm giving you the benefit of the doubt right now, but if you hurt my best friend, I will fuck you up, got it?"

Elijah slowly arches a brow. "Your friend was the one who wanted to see me, so you ask her."

"I don't care *who* said *what!*" Naomi's all serious as she wiggles a finger in his face. "You hurt her, I'll fuck you up! Understood?"

Manhattan's hustle and bustle rushes over their brief silence.

"Understood," Elijah growls. Taking a step closer to her on the sidewalk, he clenches his jaw. "But just so you know, I've never hurt a woman in my entire life, and I never *ever* will."

"You're fucking lucky I believe you." Naomi shoots him one final death glare before coming back to me.

She wraps her arms around my waist and kisses my cheeks, all while Elijah and I never take our eyes off each other. "You know what to do if he becomes difficult. Just call me, okay? I love you, girlfriend."

"I love you too, babe."

The second she walks back into the luxury apartment complex, it's just Elijah and me, and our stare-off. He steps back until he's by his vintage Camaro and pops open the passenger door, all while never taking his eyes off me. His hand steadies above the hood, leaning against it as his fingers begin to drum a rhythm that I feel plunges face-first into my heart.

He's waiting, waiting for me.

Cars that can't get past in the street because of him double parked begin honking, their extended deafening beeps doing nothing to Elijah, who stands composed, confident, and cocky.

Determined to prove to him that I too have changed since we last saw each other, I stride up to him like it's the catwalk of my life. My heels come to a halt just before I step into the passenger seat to glance up at Elijah with a glare of my own.

"If you piss me off..." I warn, fending off my nerves with clenched fists. "I *will* kick you in the balls, okay?"

Elijah stares.

And stares.

And stares.

Those gunmetal gray eyes send me to hell right here in the middle of Manhattan as the slightest half-smirk works up his lips.

"Nice seeing you too," he mockingly murmurs under his breath. "Nothing sweet about you these days, *Peaches.*"

"Damn straight there isn't."

"Mmhmmm." Elijah nods, glancing into the distance before knocking on the car's roof twice.

Those wolfish gray eyes find mine and when they do, they darken as he gestures to his car.

"So, how is this gonna go, Rosalia Philips? Are you gonna get in, or do I gotta carry you in myself?"

Chapter
SIX

Rosalia

After slipping into Elijah's tan leather passenger seat, I slam the car door in his face. You'll be happy to know that I actually complied and got inside his car without him having to touch me (which, by the way, I *wouldn't* have been opposed to any other night but tonight).

I'm pissed off with Elijah Diesel. Actually, I'm livid. Nobody in their right mind ignores somebody for two months straight, no matter what goes down. It's deceitful. Disrespectful. And something his mother should have taught him better.

As I click on my seat belt and Elijah rounds

the car, I hate how much the fight in my body begins to slip at this lingering scent. His car smells so good—exactly like him—and that musky, sandalwood blend with a hint of tobacco is everywhere.

I've never been in an upcoming rock star's car before, but Elijah has a habit of making me break all the rules, so I'm not surprised by this one.

Elijah's vintage Chevrolet Camaro is by far the most impressive thing I've ever seen. Everything is so neat. Organized. Perfect—like the restored original dash. There isn't any piled-up junk, wrappers, or thrown clothes anywhere. It's impeccable.

There isn't even an inch of dirt on the car mats.

Who even is this guy?

My body is highly aware of Elijah's presence when he pops his door open and slides into the driver's seat. He slams it shut with a clenched jaw, never looking at me once as he pulls out a cigarette.

I gawk at him for far more than I should as he lights his cigarette, lets out an appeased moan, and slips on his seat belt. In. That. Exact. Order. I think my ovaries just exploded at the sound of that gravelly moan, just saying.

Dear God.

I cross my legs, the growing heat between my thighs only intensifying the longer I watch him.

"Staring at me ain't gonna do shit to aid the gravity of this situation," Elijah mumbles under his breath, clouds of thick white smoke filling the air as he begins driving down the beautifully lit city streets.

I scrunch up my nose at the smoke. "I'm not staring."

"Oh, is that why I can feel your eyes still on me?"

I'm just staring at your beauty, jackass.

Why do boys always have the best long lashes?

And why does he look even hotter driving with one hand on the wheel? His other hand is pulled back, elbow leaning by the window as he slowly rubs a hand over his sexy dark stubble.

I scoff. "Are you always such a perpetual idiot, or is this performance just for me?"

And then something happens.

Something I never expected.

Elijah grins.

Grins.

And gah, where have those dimples been hiding all this time?

Elijah's pretty gray eyes flicker to mine just as he slows at a red light. We're first at the traffic light, and if I wasn't so fascinated by how the glowing red light cuts shapes into his perfectly structured face, I would have heard what he replied.

"Umm, sorry." I clear my throat. "What did you say?"

Elijah's grin extends to a full-blown smirk. "I said *perpetual* is a big word for a girl who just came out of pre-k."

Ugh!

I roll my eyes in frustration and stare out the window at absolutely nothing. "Can you stop teasing me about my age? I'm honestly only fifteen years younger. That's nothing."

"No, it's *everything*," he grits, and *hello, Mr. Cold as ice*. "It's everything when you're only fucking seventeen."

"You say it like it's a crime!"

"I say it like you shouldn't be in my car at this hour!"

"Seriously?" I spit, facing him just as the light turns green and he takes off. "Are you serious right now? *You're* the one who wanted to see me tonight. I was adamant in asking you for *a* date to meet, *not* for it to be *tonight*."

I don't miss the way Elijah's fist clenches around the wheel, squeezing it so tight, his knuckles turn white.

"Jesus Christ, Rosalia," he growls, and this time I feel it cut into my ego. He continuously flickers his gaze between me and the road. "How the fuck did you expect me to react after the photo you sent me, huh? Of course I wanted to see you right away."

"Why?"

"Don't."

"Don't, *what*?"

"Don't question something after I say it."

I give him a royal salute. "Yes, daddy."

That is until I realize what I just said to him...
daddy.

Oh. My. GOD.

Squeezing my eyes shut, I pray that I just disappear in *three... two... one.*

I open my eyes to Elijah's death glare.

Nope, still here.

I know I shouldn't be this turned on while he
clenches his jaw twice. Slowly. Sexily. But I am.

"Unless I'm fucking buried deep inside you,"
Elijah begins with a growl, his glare only darken-
ing. "In which *I'm not*, and *will not ever be*, then.
Do. Not. Fucking. Call. Me. *That.* Again."

My jaw drops.

Ohmygod. Ohmygod. Ohmygod.

Elijah Diesel just said that.

I think it's fair to say that after the stare-off he
has with me, the one that results in him looking
even more broody and me even more flustered, the
fact that we don't speak for the entire ride (to wher-
ever the heck we're going) is justified.

His words replay in my mind, over and over
again, until he pulls his car into park at West 36th

Street in front of what looks like a studio… a music studio hangout?

Elijah kills the engine, but that's all that happens as we both continue staring out the windshield, the silent tension desperately needing to be cut with a knife.

He just keeps taking long drags of his cigarette, like this isn't affecting him at all.

"So, what's your band called?" I ask, attempting to deflect. "Do you have a manager? Record label? I think I should know before going in… yeah?"

His eyes find mine, almost shocked. "You really want to know?"

"Of course I do."

Elijah gazes away from me. His response only comes after he's taken a few more puffs of his cigarette, its amber tip our only light at this stage, aside from the silvery moonlight pouring through the windows.

"We're an upcoming band. That's why we were in *Rolling Stone* magazine. For exposure. We do have a manager, but right now until the right label comes along, we're enjoying the indie game. This is our own private studio where we practice, record, and just hang out. No one else occupies it. We own it," Elijah quietly explains. "What else did you ask?"

"What your band is called?"

"It used to be called *Odyssey*, but a month ago we came to a unanimous decision to change it."

"Oh, why's that?"

Elijah sighs, and it's a heavy one. Loaded. "Rebranding and shit, you know."

Something tells me it's more than that, but I let it go.

"So, what's your rock band called now?"

Elijah plays with a piece of loose string on his jeans, and when his dark eyes flicker to mine, pooling in something I can't quite explain, it's so intense, I gasp.

"*Diesel Rose*," he murmurs, looking at me for the longest time as if I'm supposed to understand something.

Diesel Rose.

Elijah *Diesel.*

Diesel.

And the 'Rose'?

Could it be that the greatest love of his life was or is called 'Rose'?

Think, Rosalia, think.

Wait… wait a minute.

Rosalia Philips.

Rosalia.

Rosa.

Rose.

Diesel *Rose.*

Diesel Rose.

My breath slows.

Could it be that…?

I internally shake my head to myself. No, there's no way. Ironic, maybe. But there's no way in the world that Elijah named his band after me.

He hates me, remember? Well, he certainly did a month ago, anyway.

Diesel Rose… It's the most beautiful, most tragically bittersweet band name I've ever heard. And I love it, for all the wrong reasons.

Deciding it's best to move on from this conversation, I deflect it the best I can.

"I didn't mean to…" I pause, gulping down my pride as I manage to come up with the right words. "What I meant to say earlier was in reference to the father kind of *daddy*, not *daddy* in the sexual kind of way. Sorry, I didn't mean to unlock your… I don't know… *kink*?"

Elijah practically slams his head against the headrest. "It's not a fucking kink, Rosalia," he hisses.

"The way you shut me down, it's obvious that it is."

"Should you be talking to a thirty-one-year-old man like that?"

Thirty-one.

"I don't know. Should you be staring at a seventeen-year-old's legs like that?"

I only said it to stir him up for catching him staring because there's nothing illegal about what he's doing. About what we're *both* doing. Whatever is going on between us, it's legal. The age of consent in New York is seventeen. If I really wanted to sleep with him, I could. It doesn't make it illegal, just forbidden. Very, very forbidden. *And risky.*

And yet, here, while two o'clock blankets the ominous New York Midtown skies through the windshield window, it's Elijah Diesel's hot stare on my legs that gives me a little life.

He notices what I said because the moment I say it, his eyes leave me and it almost makes me feel hollow inside.

I slowly turn to him, surprised his eyes are squeezed shut, almost as if it's killing him not to stare, but his pride is way too big to tell me.

I stare at his cigarette, how he lines it up to the center of his soft lips as he takes another hit.

"You can look at me if you want to," I find myself whispering. "I won't tell anybody."

"Looking at you ain't good for my sanity, *Peaches.*"

Peaches.

I chew on my lower lip. "Why?"

"Because I still haven't forgiven you for what you said to me two months ago. You think I don't remember, huh?" Elijah almost scoffs. "Because

I remember it all right. I remember it well. No amount of those fucking sexy long legs of yours will make me forget."

And just like that, the walls come crumbling down. My lips part to nothingness and Elijah roughly opens his driver's door and steps out of the car, slamming it behind him.

I watch him confidently stride around the car, crush his cigarette under his Doc Martens, and not once acknowledging my existence beyond opening my door for me.

With a pang in my chest, I awkwardly thank him and step out of the car, placing a mental note in my mind that while he is an asshole, he does, oddly enough, have a slight chivalrous side. And I do mean *slight* because when he locks his car before unlocking the studio door with a code, he strides in first and the door almost slams in my face before I jump inside.

He locks it shut after me.

There isn't much more I can say other than, "*whoa*," when my eyes rake the space beyond Elijah. A long hallway with dark walls is what we're met with, cool vintage band posters aligning the wall with small lights above each poster like it's an art museum. It's as if those posters are inspiration for where Diesel Rose wants to be, and to be honest, I love it.

The warm lighting feeds into the atmosphere as I follow Elijah down the hall.

The Ramones.

Led Zeppelin.

K.I.S.S.

My favorite, *The Neighbourhood*.

This place is like heaven.

We come to the end of the hall and my feet slow by the dark oak hardwood floors. There are two options—left or right—and both are masked off with solid black doors.

I glance up at Elijah and he slightly glances over his shoulder at me. "Do you want to meet the boys first and then talk?"

I shrug, failing to ask him *what boys exactly* because I'm just so mesmerized by this space. I knew he was going to take me somewhere to talk. I just didn't expect it to be *here*—in his livelihood.

Elijah turns left and I follow him like a lost puppy. He knocks on the dark door twice, and when nothing happens, he lets out a curse word and presses his thumb against a security thing beside the door. A red light switches to green and the door automatically pops open.

Gritty bass guitar going wild, impressive drumming, and a low but passionate argument fill the room as Elijah steps into his throne of a studio room.

The first question pops into my head. "How did you expect anybody to open the door if it's supposed to be soundproof?"

"The door has sensors. A buzz rings inside this studio when somebody knocks twice, but these fuckers were probably too high to notice."

High?

He continues walking, but when he realizes I'm just standing here, turns around and presses a hand by my lower back, encouraging me in.

"You sure these guys won't kill me?" I whisper over to him with a side-eye, bouncing on my heels with both nerves and excitement.

Elijah dramatically rolls his eyes. "I'm in a rock band, Rosalia, not the damn mafia."

"What's the difference, big fella, huh? I've heard the saying sex, drugs, and rock and roll before… the mafia can't be too different. Well, I guess violence and live ammunition in exchange for rock and roll, but still! Hey, wait up! Where are you going?"

Elijah ignores me completely and keeps on walking.

Note taken.

I jump when the door dead bolts shut behind me and I run after him, feeding more into that lost puppy personification.

The vibes in here are honestly so damn cool. Epic exposed brick walls. Continued oak floors.

Large angled Persian rugs. Everything feeds into the leather, steel, and pops of brass vibes I imagined for this place. Full-on rock and roll industrial in the best kind of way.

The studio is huge, like double the size of the first level of my brownstone with a main chill-out practice area, then farther along there's a soundproof glass recording studio. And a little farther down, a lounge area with brown leather buttoned couches and a black mini fridge.

The air is laced with tobacco, cologne, and whiskey. It's the most masculine combination I've ever smelled, which as three sets of eyes flicker my way, reminds me that I'm the only woman in this room.

The music comes to a slaughtering end and three guys who look like they just stepped out of MFWFR—Milan Fashion Week for Rockers (and yes, I did just make that up)—stare at me. Like a real-deep-into-my-soul-until-there's-complete-nothingness-left-inside-me stare.

I silently scream to myself.

Is this a bad time to admit that I don't do too well with meeting new people?

Elijah steps up beside me. "Guys, this is *Peaches*. You can call her Rosalia."

The drummer—who seems the most standoffish out of all of them—is the first one to slightly nod. He has a leather French type of beret on, but with spikes instead of bows. He's wearing full-on leather. Leather jeans. Leather shirt. Leather jacket. Did I forget to mention it's hardcore summer? I'm pretty sure if I could see his shoes behind the drums, they'd also be leather.

Everywhere I look, I get extra tough guy vibes from him; his gaze, the dark ink crawling up his neck, and his luscious long chestnut hair, which reaches his ribs with golden streaks, that my mother—if she saw—would admire for six hours straight.

"Nice to meet ya, Rosalia." He nods, spinning a drumstick in his grip.

"Hi." I give him a tight-lipped smile.

Not really knowing what else to do, I glance back at Elijah. He keeps his gaze on the drummer but is talking to me when he says, "That's Dave, as you can see, our drummer. He's been on tour with some of the greatest." A smirk crawls up his lips. "So, he's a fucking traitor, but now he's here to stay."

"Damn straight I am." Dave chuckles.

Elijah motions to a guy with perfect caramel skin to the left of Dave—the guitarist—who actually steps forth to take my hand.

"Yo, I'm Zander." He grins. He has the prettiest brown eyes with violet brush field spots I've ever seen, lined in heavy eyeliner. "Sick skirt."

I glance down at the short denim pleated skirt

Naomi picked out for me and return my gaze to him, grinning. "Thanks, my best friend picked it out for me even though it was in my closet."

"Epiccc. Well then, I want to meet this friend of yours too now."

I find myself giggling because this wasn't what I was expecting Elijah's bandmates to be like at all. I thought they'd be all metal rock heads with death glares and flip me off whenever they got the chance. Instead, they're actually good guys, despite them all being tough rockers.

Okay, maybe these guys aren't murderers. Maybe it's just Elijah Diesel.

Speaking of... Elijah steps closer to me and his cologne floods my lungs, cuing all my damn butterflies as he clears his throat, slaughtering the laughter between Zander and me.

Zander awkwardly coughs and steps back, collecting his guitar from the Persian rug.

"Last guy..." Elijah mumbles, like he really hates doing this, and gestures toward a guy with a bass guitar strapped to his chest who's looking everywhere but me. "That's Knives."

Knives?

Just as I'm about to speak, Knives—who's smoking a rolled-up joint—pulls up his hoodie, covering his short dirty-blond locks. He grumbles something under his breath, and I only catch my name alongside a profanity before he continues typing away on his phone.

Well, two out of three ain't bad.

I turn to Elijah, perplexed. "Did you just say *Knives*? Is that his real name?"

"It's an acronym of the first three letters of his first name and the last three letters of his surname. *Kni*ght I*ves*. We just call him Knives."

"Whoa, that's actually cool, Elijah."

"The fuck?" Knives scoffs, his voice not as deep as I imagined. He flicks his light eyes to me, completely motionless. "Did you just fucking say *Elijah*?"

I stare at him with bile rushing up my throat. He's by far the scariest here and… maybe isn't a serial killer but could definitely be a psychopath for all I know. Especially when he starts chuckling.

I rock on the balls of my feet, my palms getting sweaty because suddenly four guys who are practically strangers are staring at me at two o'clock in the morning and I'm taking way too long at a simple question. It feels like I'm drowning in the waves of the Atlantic with no way out.

Is this guy playing with me, or did he just not hear?

"Yeah…" I say, finally finding my voice. "Why?"

He eyes Elijah and a smirk slowly crawls. "Thought you only went by Diesel, bro, no?"

Silence takes over the room.

I furrow my brows… *Am I missing something?*

I glance at Elijah, who is clenching his jaw at his bass guitarist with the devil in his eyes. "Shut the fuck up, Knives."

Knives simply shrugs and turns to me with a yawn before that smirk resurfaces from the apparent shadows of his dark heart. "Nice to meet you, Rosalia. You sing or something?"

"Umm, I dance ballet actually."

Dave and Zander glance at each other and snicker.

Shutting his phone, Knives lets out a hum and sizes me up. "Professionally and shit?"

"I would love to when I graduate, but my father would probably prefer me to do something in lieu of his profession."

Elijah—Diesel—or whatever the heck he wants me to call him, crosses his arms over his broad chest and for the first time since we've entered this room, looks at me for more than two seconds. "Which is?"

"Medicine." I nervously smile. "My father's a neurosurgeon."

They're really beautiful guys, but Elijah—*gah*—there's just something extra about him. Maybe it's the mystery in his eyes, and how it comes with such sexiness, alongside the fact that he's the lead vocalist, but there's something really special about him.

It's crazy how we went from a tense argument in his late '60s vintage Chevrolet Camaro moments to him… introducing me to his bandmates. But I'm sure the convo Elijah and I need to have after this won't be as pretty.

"Oh, shit," Knives curses and he takes another drag of the joint, its toxic smoke lingering as he waves it up in the air. "Promise it's prescription."

"I'm sure it is."

"Soooo, how do you and Diesel know each other?"

My heart simmers into silence as I open and close my mouth like a fish. *Do I tell him the truth? That I was stalking Elijah/Diesel like a nutcase?* I'm lost for words because that doesn't give the greatest impression of myself, even though it is the truth.

Besides, it's not like Elijah and I are even friends… or lovers… So, what are we?

Does Knives genuinely not know how we met? Or did Elijah tell his bandmate about me, about how we met and is Knives now just testing me?

It would mean this introduction would be a lie.

Before I can make even more of a fool out of myself, Elijah Diesel simmers the silence with his raspy honeyed sin voice. "*Peaches* ain't answering, so it's question fucking skipped."

Elijah didn't tell them. At all.

"All right." Knives sighs, strumming a few notes

on his bass, and it sounds so damn good. "Last question I have for right now. You know how you said you still wanted to dance when you graduate, but you probably should do something in more the medical fucking realm, yeah?"

"Yeah…"

"Well, what undergrad are you currently taking? And I warn you, answer carefully."

"Oh." I gasp and shake my head to clear the confusion. "I meant when I graduate *high school*, not *college*… I'm seventeen. I'll be starting my senior year when summer ends."

I knew my clarification would do some damage, but I didn't expect *this…*

"SEVENTEEN?!" Knives shouts, and not only do his eyes widen when he snaps his head to Elijah, but the others do too. "DIESEL, DUDE! What the FUCK? She hasn't even GRADUATED HIGH SCHOOL YET?"

His words echo in my mind, but all I hear is, *unworthy, unworthy, unworthy.*

"Shut your *fucking* mouth, Knives, before I shut it for you!" Elijah growls, shoving Knives's chest back when he steps forward. "*Peaches* and I are gonna have a little chat. In private. None of you find a way to sneak into the bar unless you want your balls severed."

"I like you, Rosalia, but I wouldn't sacrifice my

balls for you," the drummer, Dave, mumbles under his breath as he hits his drumsticks together five times. "You're on your own."

And the drumming commences but does nothing to drown out my rapidly beating heart that rushes into overdrive. I don't like the way his bandmates are looking at me—Knives in particular—he's got a look in his eyes that tells me I don't belong here. With them. With Elijah.

Wordlessly, Elijah slips his hand in mine and we're out of the room in seconds. Any other time I'd be giddy, but after what just happened, I feel like curling up in a fetal position and never talking to any of these guys again.

Elijah doesn't let his tight grip on my hand go as we cross the hall to the only other door. It's only after the door clicks unlocked and we step in that our intertwined hands fall.

Holy... *wow, this place is so cool.*

This room is the exact size of the other but done up like a bar. The same exposed brick walls and oak floorboards, but for some reason, the ceilings seem taller. Frosted floor-to-ceiling black steel New York windows take over one wall, and I love the warm Edison pendant lights Elijah flicks on. There are so many of them and they cascade down on a thin metal rope, matching the industrial theme.

The bar's countertop is a soft charcoal marble,

and instead of tables and chairs surrounding the room, brown leather studded couches, some buttoned like the one in the studio. It's the type of luxurious bar you would host a function, not have inside your studio, but I go for it.

Behind the counter is a lit-up wall filled with all kinds of liquor on brass shelves, and I really like how the two red neon signs above the bar glowing, DIESEL ROSE, and then lower down, Sex, Drugs, and Rock and Roll, gives the entire room a soft, devilish hue.

The second neon sign has me laughing inside. I said those exact words to Elijah when we entered this building, and I questioned the difference between his rock band and the underworld.

Feeling defeated, I watch as Elijah steps into the bar with tense shoulders. Although we never did start off in a good mood tonight, it feels like the air between us has become far worse.

So maybe it's the devil in me that makes me want to sin a little when Elijah spreads his hands firmly on the countertop, flicks his dark gaze to me, and not so calmly says, "You wanted to talk—*talk*."

But I invite it.

Livid, I don't stop giving him a piece of my mind from ten feet away. I tell him how much of a jerk he is for thinking he can act so nonchalant after ignoring me for two months. I tell him that if I could go back in time, I'd slap his face for even suggesting coming inside of my house, instead of simply giving me my schoolbag on the porch steps.

I tell him that I never meant to call him a *freak* and that it's been eating me up inside ever since.

That I finished *The Beautiful and Damned* weeks ago, and how rude it was to never return my calls. Then I question why he left me such a heartfelt book for a man so cruel.

I tell him everything.

Everything. Everything. Everything.

Including how frustrated I am that these things keep on happening to me. That people keep fucking up my emotions. Abandoning me—including him.

I tell him the thought of graduating next year makes me sick because I don't know what the hell I want to do with my life.

I tell him I'm sorry. I'm sorry for offending him and causing so much pain.

I tell him I never want to see him again, and then I tell him that I do because for some reason I really like seeing him. Being around him makes me feel different... noticed... *seen*.

And then, when I'm on my last breath and am sure I'll either burst into a million pieces or pass out from all my lack of breathing, I give him an ultimatum—*to either stay in my life forever or to leave forever*—because there isn't an in-between for me.

Through all my shouts, Elijah doesn't move a muscle. He remains standing tall with all the space between us. Defiant. And while I'm here panting, trying to catch my breath, he. Freaking. Does. *Nothing.*

He just stares.

Stares.

Stares.

Until the onyx-gray coating his pretty eyes gleams in a reckless desire for neither life nor death. It's as if he has me hanging onto purgatory by a bare thread with the way his piercing gaze punctures me.

I have never—nor will I ever—meet a man as complicated as Elijah Diesel.

It has me ball up my fight. Grind my jaw. Stride up to him with my cherry-red stilettos and demand he tells me something. *Anything.*

I'm so fired up that when he eventually angles his body my way so we're both behind the counter, separated by a few inches, even more blood rumbles up my veins.

The stare-off doesn't end, not even when he begins to grind his teeth and blindly reaches for an open bottle of whiskey on the counter that I didn't notice before.

"I'm going to kill you for being so freaking cruel to me!" I grit, slamming my hand on the cold marble counter. "*Kill! You!* Elijah Diesel!"

He doesn't flinch, but I sure hurt my hand on the solid Italian stone.

Elijah does everything but give me a response as he arches a brow, his eyes darkening even deeper when he brings the whiskey bottle to his lips like a beast. He gulps down two fingers' worth, all without ever taking his gaze off me over the glass.

Like a true rocker, he doesn't even care to wipe his mouth after he slams the bottle back on the counter, making me flinch, alongside my heart.

And I hate it.

Hate *him*.

Hate him even more as my eyes settle on the remnants of the amber liquid coating his lips, enticed with the way it has his mouth glimmering in the low light. Between the warm hue of the Edison lights and the seductive glow of the red neons, Elijah Diesel, my gorgeous villain, becomes a wonderland I wish I could just wrap my body around and kiss. Devour. Love on until he tells me to stop.

It's one way to finally get him to speak to me.

It's one way to stop this silent cat-and-mouse game.

It's one way to know if the coldest melancholic-eyed rocker would kiss me back…

I've never been kissed before, and right now, as the air between us thickens, that same devil in me craves making Elijah Diesel my first. To let kissing him be that wild thing I do this summer.

I crave it.

I crave having his soft lips on mine. For him to kiss me back. Hard. Like he hates me.

I crave it like I do my next breath, which is why I lean forth and do exactly that…

I kiss the monster I've secretly prayed would crawl out from under my bed ever since he stormed out of my bedroom months ago. I kiss Elijah Diesel—the wicked devil—breathlessly.

Chapter
SEVEN

Rosalia

The second my lips crash against his, I know I'm a goner for all the wrong reasons.

I'm nervous. So damn nervous, I feel the trembles all up my spine as my heart kicks into overdrive, but it's that same adrenaline rush that propels me to hell's gates.

With my clammy hands awkwardly pressed against his chest, his hot breath tickles my cheek the second I slam my mouth against his. The sparks in my chest intensifying. Suddenly, I'm grateful for all the *Cosmopolitan* magazines Naomi and I used to read detailing how to give the most breathtaking kiss.

I'm not desperate. I'm a flustered seventeen-year-old melting against Elijah Diesel's soft lips. They're warm. *So warm.* Everything I wasn't expecting.

I kiss him slow, adamant, with everything that's in me, all while he remains motionless with what I sense is a vicious clenched jaw. He punishes me by not kissing me back.

I repeat...

Elijah. Diesel. Does. Not. Kiss. Me. Back.

He doesn't press me up against him.

He doesn't give me a sign that he wants this.

He doesn't part his lips, rejecting anything deeper.

Instead, he taunts me, like the cold-hearted beast he is, making me feel even smaller all while I rake my hand through his dark wavy hair, needing him closer.

My lips mold against his, sparks igniting my entire body because I've never been this daring before. Not with an older man I barely know. My heart slams against my ribcage so recklessly, panicking during this one-sided breathless kiss.

I kiss him hard. Endlessly. But it all amounts to nothing.

Shit. Shit. Shit.

I'm certain it can't get more awkward than this when I abruptly pull away.

Ohmygod, this is so embarrassing.

I just wasted my first kiss on a man who PURPOSELY didn't even MOVE A MUSCLE IN PROTEST just to show HE'S THE ONE WINNING this invisible game between us.

Because he's doing just that—*winning*—and it's only confirmed when I pull away with shameful eyes and Elijah's glare is indifferent. It's so obvious that he's the one who calls the shots.

He's so vain, he didn't even kiss me back.

God, I feel so pathetic.

It doesn't matter how blurry my gaze becomes. I hold back tears. There's no way I'm crying in front of him. *Because* of him. I won't. No matter how much of a painstaking reminder my smeared glossy lipstick on his lips is of my foolish action mere seconds ago.

Finally—FINALLY—after what feels like fifteen minutes since Elijah last spoke, he says a word. Well, he says more, but I suddenly wish he could have stopped at the one.

"*Peaches*," Elijah rasps, and there's fury in his gaze, a deadly devilish fire, one I wish didn't just ignite right before my very eyes. "You shouldn't have kissed me."

Elijah takes a step toward me.

I take one back.

He takes another two steps forward.

I take two back.

He starts striding confidently, like a wolf wanting to claim what's his again.

Flustered, I rush backward and accidentally slam against the bar's exposed brick wall, chilling coldness trickling down my spine. A hiss escapes my lips at the force.

Ouch.

In a flash, Elijah has me properly pinned against the wall, his hips locking me in with nowhere to go. He towers over me, an entire foot of height difference. Frustrated, I attempt to shove him back, but his reflexes are so fast, he roughly grips my wrists with one hand before I make any contact with his chest.

A crazed growl escapes his lips and the grip on my wrists tightens as he slams them against the wall, above my head.

The action is hot. Demanding. *Dominant.* It's also the complete undoing for me because from this moment forth, I know I don't have the upper hand like I did earlier.

No, not anymore.

Not after I virtually smothered him in unreturned kisses and died from mortification.

Elijah's wicked glare slowly forms into a

slow, sexy half-smirk, but a condescending one nonetheless.

"Rosalia, tell me something..." he begins softly, and then the smirk flickers to complete carnage with every staccato growl—a sickly reminder of how fast his mood can alter. "What. The. *Fuck.* Was. That?"

Hyperventilating inside, I stare back at him with wide eyes. My body is numb. My throat is dry. I have no words.

I'm so screwed.

"Ohhh, you're not going to speak now, huh? You think if you keep quiet, I won't talk?"

"I..." A staggered breath escapes me. "I, umm—"

"ANSWER ME!" Elijah yells, slamming his free hand against the exposed brick, missing my face by inches. "WHAT THE *FUCK* WERE YOU DOING *KISSING ME*?"

Shaking away some of my blonde waves that blew into my face when his fist hit the wall, I shut my eyes to the soundtrack of Elijah's heavy breaths.

This thing some people call a heart jolts—*just like it always does around him.* It scares me how much I'm still drawn to this even when he's like this. When he's pinning me up against the wall, bounding my wrists, and yelling in my face asking why I kissed him.

I have nothing but the truth—*my* truth—to give to him. Nothing else.

"I really hate the way I feel so nervous whenever I'm around you, the nervous that brings butterflies to my stomach… like right now," I whisper, barely hearing my own words myself as my eyes remain shut. "This adrenaline… I've been wanting to feel it for a long time, but now that I finally do, I don't know how to feel about it."

Elijah remains silent. His crazed breaths, lingering cologne, and warmth of his body pressed against mine remind me this isn't a tragic dream or bittersweet nightmare. He's here.

I continue, "At the start of summer, I made this stupid goal for myself to do something wild before August ends. I made the goal to prove I…" A lump forms at the back of my throat, drilling ache into my ocean of angst. "To prove I was worth it, and that I have what it takes to be free. I kissed you because I thought it would mean you would finally talk to me after everything I just said to you. I did it because kissing you is just about the wildest thing I could ever do."

The words that have been chained to my chest are finally out. I don't know how Elijah will take it, but all I do know is that there's nothing else I can say to explain myself. That was all of it.

I know kissing Elijah Diesel was foolish, but the way he reacted was as if I'd killed him.

I just want him to understand.

"*Fuck.*" Elijah sighs and shocks me with how intimately low his voice becomes. "You don't want that, *Peaches*, believe me. You don't want to be kissing me."

With my heartbeat in my throat, right beside that lump, I flicker my eyes open. I wasn't sure what I would be getting, but gazing up into Elijah's eyes now as he lowers his head so we're level, I see the change in them. The fury is gone, and in its place—nothing. Just wolfish onyx.

I want to lick my lipstick off his lips, bite his lip, and then slap him.

"I did," I confess with a frown. "I *do*."

"You *don't*," Elijah grits. "You're smart, Rosalia, so don't be this naïve. You're seventeen. I'm fifteen years older. What do you think will happen at the end of the summer, hmm? That you'd change me, we'd fall in love, and go running off into the sunset together?"

He cocks his head at my delayed response.

I shake my head. "I'm not saying that's going to happen, but—"

He cuts me off, "No *buts*. It ain't happening. Why? Because Elijah Diesel doesn't fall in love."

Elijah's grip tightens on my wrists, all while his other hand slowly comes down to give my lacy choker the gentlest of tugs.

Oh.

His gaze lowers to his finger, which squeezes beneath the tightest gap between the white lace and my throat, looping it, almost fascinated as he traces the detailing.

My breaths labor at just how close we're standing. I swear he can feel every pulse of my heart with his finger pressed up against me.

"I don't fall in love." Fixing his eyes back on me, he smolders and roughly inches me even closer with a tug of the choker that our noses brush. "Not even with self-acclaimed good girls who are actually bad girls wearing my weakness so fucking well."

I gasp.

I knew he'd like the choker.

His smolder deepens.

"And believe me," Elijah adds in a murmur. "I'm not saying this just to be all fucking broody. I'm saying it because you're seventeen and should know better than to be with me at this hour."

My jaw drops. *Is this guy for real? Does he seriously think he can spin this all around?*

Liar.

I don't believe his words for one second, and for the first time since he pinned me against this wall, I find my voice and tell him exactly how it is.

"Oh my God, will you stop being so hypocritical, Elijah?" I spit, narrowing my gaze with a frustrated scream. "*You* are the one who wanted to meet *me* at this hour!"

"Because you wouldn't fucking leave me alone!"

"Well, we both wouldn't be here if you didn't storm out of my bedroom like a darn hurricane."

"If you kept your insults to yourself, that wouldn't have happened."

"Oh my God, I get it, but I literally apologized to you!" I practically scream. "*Twice!*"

"Still doesn't change the fact you're only seventeen."

"For the love of God, will you stop with the age? I'm not dumb. I know what I'm doing. Besides, if you were to bend me over right this second and make love to me, which I wouldn't be opposed to, it would be legal. New York's age of consent is seventeen."

Bend me over. Make love to me. Wouldn't be opposed to.

I squeeze my eyes shut, mortified. *Oh. My. God.*

Yep. I just said that. Out loud. Not in my head.

You're such an idiot for speaking your mind, Rosalia.

Elijah's lips part to nothing, pause, and then violently shut closed.

Check-freaking-mate.

Silence laces the air, blanketing with a fizzled tension neither of us can avoid.

Desire. Hatred. Curiosity.

"Rosalia Philips." A slow, devilish darkness hangs on the edges of Elijah's lips. "Did you just say you want me to fuck you?"

Yes.

Time slows. I bite my lower lip and those onyx wonderlands flicker there.

Even through all this heated rage, am I still that obvious to him?

Well, I mean, you did just openly verbally admit it, Rosalia, so there's that.

I scoff to hide the blush crawling up my cheeks. "That's not what I meant."

Elijah arches a brow. "But you just admitted you want me, right?"

I look away, my answer evident from my silence... *Yes. Yes, I want you, asshole.*

Elijah Diesel—my melancholic addiction—growls. Like full-on sexily growls, almost on the verge of a moan. And just like that, the fury returns.

"*First*," Elijah spits, his touch by my throat leaving to hold a finger up in front of my face. "I don't make love. I fuck. *Rough*." He holds up another finger. "*Second*, I'm not going to fuck you, *Peaches*, so get that lust out of your eyes."

I can't look at him anymore. It hurts so much. It hurts to keep looking at somebody who makes your heart feel like it's going to burst out of your chest and him being so damn cold.

Elijah lets go of my wrists and I let them fall freely to my sides, not daring to move. Suddenly, those Edison pendant lights seem so important as I stare at them with blurry eyes like they're my cure.

"If you fucking try that again, try to kiss me, I will never speak to you again. Is that fucking understo—"

"No, it isn't, Diesel," I grit, cutting him off. "That's what you really prefer, isn't it—*Diesel*?"

His eyes flicker between mine. "Why are you doing this?"

"Doing *what*?"

"Fuckin' with my head. What the fuck do you want from me, little girl?"

"For you not to act like an ass after my epic fail of a first kiss."

Elijah laughs darkly in my face. "Oh, please, that wasn't your first kiss."

"It. Was. My. First. Kiss."

The laughter is slaughtered by a glare. "That's the most foolish thing I've ever heard."

"Wow, spoken like a true gentleman who reads F. Scott Fitzgerald. You're unbelievable, Elijah. I wish I had never kissed you, asshole!"

"Good. Because it was your first and last time kissing me."

"You're so confident you won't ever be in love with anybody, aren't you?" I hiss. "Well, I hope the girl of your dreams walks into your life, that you adore her with everything you've got, and then when you need her the most, she breaks your goddamn heart."

"That girl is you, *Peaches*, except you won't be the one to break my heart. Trust me."

"Fuck you!" I scream, and it gets harder to hold the tears when I shove his hard chest back.

Not expecting it, he stumbles back for a second, and the next thing I know, I'm being pinned up against the wall again with his hand roughly gripping my throat, and then... *he* kisses *me*.

Oh.

My.

God.

Elijah Diesel is kissing *me*. Hard. Recklessly. Far more breathlessly than I ever could.

I hate myself for wanting him.

I hate myself for caring.

I hate myself for kissing him back, letting him devour me in ways only devils know how.

My lips move in rhythm with his and my hands automatically return to weave through his hair and tug on the tips, while his free hand cups my face tight. Elijah Diesel's kiss is lethal, filthy— toxic, in the best kind of way. I can't get enough of the way our lips move so recklessly in sync.

Whoa.

His tongue caresses the center of my lips, in the gentlest of ways amid his recklessness. Our tongues collide like vicious fires, every single filthy stroke like heaven on earth with Lucifer.

A moan escapes my throat at how good it feels to be kissed by Elijah, and he must feel its loud vibration ricochet through my throat because his hold on it intensifies.

His grip is so dominating, so kinky, and something I'm really coming to love. Restraint. I can barely breathe in the sexualized chokehold, yet it's his passionate French kisses that revive me, again and again and again.

Elijah tastes like the sweetest peppermint and the darkest of whiskeys. There's also a hint of tobacco on his tongue, and it's all three of those things combined that has my warm sex continue to throb in arousal.

My poor excuse of a kiss minutes ago wasn't my first—*this* is my first kiss—and he knows it.

Elijah continues taking control, a moan vibrating through him too now as our tongues continue melting together, every hungered kiss turning even more desperate. Crazed. He consumes me. Completely. In ways I never knew existed.

It's so euphoric.

So addictive.

Bittersweet—because I know this will never happen again.

And it's only confirmed when Elijah abruptly ends our kiss, coming back for more with two more final pecks. The last lingers, even after he sexily tugs down my lower lip, nibbling it softly like I'm his. Then, only after I moan out his name, he pulls away from me completely.

I instantly miss his touch. His heat. His kiss.

A darkened desire I know shouldn't be there is still so evident in his gaze when he stares down at me with heavy breaths, realizing what he just did. Our exhales merge together. He lets go of my throat and catching my breath has never felt more essential with the way my lungs burn in protest.

I ache for more. Ache for him. Ache for our tattered story.

Elijah Diesel was supposed to be a gorgeous rocker I admired in *Rolling Stone* magazine; he was never supposed to become a real-life fantasy that has changed my life in these months. He's all I think about, and I know it's wrong, but I really want to start fresh. I don't want him to be looking at me like he is right now, with so much… regret.

Then everything. Just. Softens. Down.

It gets quieter.

Intimate.

It feels as if we can look at each other without the world exploding in our faces.

"Rosalia…" Elijah murmurs softly. "Did you see the *Rolling Stone* magazine article I was in?"

I gulp down, suffering from a little whiplash because his question is so out of left field. "Yes."

"I know you asked me the name of my band, so that kind of answers it in itself, but did you read the article?"

"No."

"Have you ever… I don't know, looked me up?"

"No."

"Why?"

"I guess I wanted to deduce my own impression of you." I sadly sigh in all my truth. "I didn't and still don't want my thoughts on you to come from that *Rolling Stone* article, the world, or what an online source says. I want to hear it all from you, Elijah. The real you."

The air crackles between us, and I worry I said too much.

I try again. "I followed you that day not because I'm some crazy stalker or some lovesick girl. I followed you because I… I don't know why. You just felt like a risk, like the one person who didn't know me and therefore didn't have to see me for all my faults and sins."

"You don't have faults and sins, *Peaches*."

"I do." I sniffle, just as the first tear slips, cascading down my cheek to the corner of my lips. "So many, and I'm sorry for everything. I didn't mean for all of this to happen. For you to hate me. I just…"

"I get it. But I can't be your cure, Rosalia. It doesn't work that way." Resting his forehead against mine, Elijah softly shakes his head. "You ever try and kiss me again, I'll ruin your life."

"Please, I—"

"Shhh, *Peaches*," Elijah softly whispers, his thumb slowly brushing over my swollen lips. He's killing me slowly with his touch as he smooths over my soft skin, wiping the tear away. "So please don't cry for me because I can't be your cure. Not in the way you need."

"Why?"

I don't get his hot and cold.

How he can be so rough, then so sweet.

It's too much.

"Because I'll break your heart," Elijah whispers by my ear, his soft kisses down my neck leaving invisible scars. "And I'll leave without ever saying goodbye. So, to answer your ultimatum, I'm staying in your life, *Peaches*, whatever the fuck it means. Just don't fuck me over, don't take this for what it isn't, 'cause if you do, I'll just fuck you over right back."

The lump in my throat finally gives way and explodes in waves of vulnerability, dragging me down.

I'm losing him before our start.

Without ever looking at me again, Elijah pulls away, stumbling back until he's leaning over the bar countertop.

There's silence, and then…

"Rosalia… I didn't mean to hurt you, or for it to go this far either."

In the pain of losing him, a small smile works up my lips. "I forgive you… and I hope you find it in you to forgive me too. For everything."

Nodding, Elijah spreads his long legs out and

downs some more whiskey before blindly throwing me his car keys from his back pocket.

I catch them, all skittish.

"Run, Rosalia," he whispers into the bottle of amber liquid, his head hung low. "Get in my car and drive the fuck home."

Confused, I shake my head, but he can't see me. "Elijah, I'm sorry. Can we please just work this out? I don't want to leave."

"You *need* to."

"But that doesn't—"

"*Please*," Elijah begs, emotion cutting in his voice as he shuts his eyes. "Please, just go. Because if I look at you again, I'll break every single promise I just made to you. Those of me ruining your life. If I look at you again even for a single second, I'll want you—just like you want me—and that, *Peaches*, that will fucking destroy us both."

And with an ache in my chest, I listen.

I run out of the bar, out of the building, and into his car.

His scent lingers in the lonely air, reminding me he shouldn't have ever meant this much to me. I don't know what comes after this. What this means for us. If I'll truly ever see Elijah again. All I do know is that when I'm with him, I feel better.

I come out of my shell.

I become the woman I want to be, without the fear of losing those I love.

Driving in his vintage Chevrolet Camaro feels odd without him. Tucking those keys underneath the doormat feels even worse. But what I hate the most as I tumble into bed, right beside a snoring Naomi, is that my heart feels bruised.

Tattered and bruised with Elijah Diesel's permanent mark.

Tattered and bruised with the taste of whiskey still on my tongue.

And if this is what it feels like with my melancholic rocker still wanting to be in my life, what would it have felt like if he said that tonight was the last time I'll ever see him again in my life?

Elijah Diesel, whatever happens next, always remember I'm yours...

Chapter
EIGHT

Elijah

*F*uckkk.

Rosalia Philips is a constant in my mind; long after she bolts out of the bar, my car's keys jiggling in her grip. It takes a solid ten minutes for me to get my shit together and finally glance up at the space she used to be—by the exposed brick wall.

Where she kissed me.

Where I kissed her ruthlessly.

Where I felt the last piece of my self-control slipping away.

Fuck. Fuck. Fuck.

I know I shouldn't have ever touched Rosalia.

Should have never devoured her. But those gorgeous light green eyes were gazing into mine with so much desire, so much need, that I ached to be the monster to cure her nightmare of a first kiss.

Jealousy took over and I showed her what a real kiss felt like… *electrifying*.

Even though Rosalia left the bar a good ten minutes ago, her lips are still bruised on mine. I haven't stopped clenching my jaw and my grip around this damn whiskey bottle. I'm so fucking angry with myself that heated tension crawls up my spine, deepening my throbbing headache.

I don't like that my heart feels so funny.

I don't like that it *feels* at all.

I've never been the kind of man to notice my own heartbeats before in a bid to silence everything that I am, but ever since I first laid my eyes upon Rosalia tonight in front of some fancy fucking apartment, the pitter-patter in my chest have kicked into overdrive.

I've been obsessed with those glossy pink lips of hers, enticed by her fierceness, and my life has been hanging on the thread with borrowed air ever since.

And my cock, which is only settling down now, has been a hard, pulsing nightmare all night.

I know *Peaches* shouldn't affect me this way.

I know it's bad.

But the second she openly admitted she wanted me, *fuckkk*, I wanted to take that peachy seventeen-year-old ass of hers and spank it hard until her skin was flushed the darkest shade of scarlet blushes. I wanted to spank her until she took the words back. All of them.

I don't know how the fuck I kept it together when I was kissing her. How I had enough control not to piston my hips forward so that she didn't feel the aching erection she brought on.

Her.

Only *her.*

I've had a difficult life. A tragically depressing one. And I know *Peaches* should stay the hell away from me, but I can't seem to fucking let her go. It's not a good thing for a man like me, a man who's barely surviving by the air in his lungs. Who can't seem to get (nor want) the taste of sweet cherry off his tongue—*the taste of her.*

As I step out of the bar and into the studio, Dave, Zander, and Knives's instrumental melodies do shit all to ease my thoughts. These late night/early morning jam sessions aren't anything new for us. These lonely hours of the night seem to be when inspiration hits the most. When corrosive liquor, illegal joints, and Diesel Rose's melancholic alternative indie rock numbs my cold, cold heart.

"The fuck happened to you, man?" Knives smirks from where he's lying down on the Persian rug, his fingers never too far from his bass guitar.

I grind my teeth.

Peaches happened.

Some confidence this guy has after all the shit he's put me through already.

Not having time for his taunts, I fucking ignore him and instead reach down to tug the rolled joint from his lips. He dramatically rolls his eyes and now I'm the one smirking.

Raking a hand through my hair, I take a drag off the joint, the instant hit bringing a little slice of bliss to the pain trapped deep inside my soul. Waves of calmness baptize my body in a way I can only describe as heaven.

I can feel all the guys' eyes on me, hot like fucking vultures just waiting for me to react. I love these guys. I really do. They're like brothers to me. We've been through hell and back together. Honestly. But right now, it's difficult. I don't feel like talking, and with my feeling obsolete anyway, they get the message without me having to say a single word.

I knew it was a fucking mistake bringing Rosalia Philips to the studio. Making her meet the band. *What the fuck was I thinking?* They'll just assume, and I don't want that. I don't want their thoughts. Not right now while I'm losing my goddamn mind.

I've never brought a girl to one of our late-night jams before, even though Rosalia didn't hear shit.

I've never introduced anybody (except my damn alter-ego) to the band before.

I've never given anybody a nickname before.

Yeah, *I'm in big fucking trouble*, and I ain't just saying it for shits and giggles.

"I don't want to talk about what you may or may not think," I say with a tense jaw, my gaze slowly stalking between the three of them while blowing out a thick, white cloud. "*Peaches* ain't my friend, lover, or acquaintance… she's simply *Peaches*. So I don't want to hear any of you motherfuckers telling me any different, 'cause you know me, I won't listen."

And then, without me waiting for them to agree, I take hold of the microphone and gold-plated stand I dropped to the floor the second I received Rosalia's text earlier tonight. It's easily my favorite stand laced in a detailed vintage snake and little rocker skulls.

I need to forget about Rosalia and what happened tonight.

I need to fucking forget it all before I deal with the consequences of giving her my prized possession to drive home—my vintage Chevrolet Camaro—something I've never allowed any soul to borrow, even for a split second, including the boys.

And that says everything in itself...

I've lost my fucking mind.

Because no matter how much I shouldn't, all I want is Peaches.

Continue Elijah and Rosalia's story in
DIESEL ROSE Now!

Also by
VANESSA LUISA

The Giannotti World:
An interconnected series of bittersweet romance
standalones set in Seattle.

Merciful Vows (#1)

DIESEL ROSE:
The poetically tragic rock star and his muse…

Remember I'm Yours (#0.5)

Diesel Rose (#1)

STANDALONES:

Oceans of Us

Kisses in Heartache

Happy reading!
Vanessa Luisa xo

About the
AUTHOR

Vanessa Luisa is a contemporary romance author. She resides in Melbourne, Australia, with her army of current reads, sassy cat, and Tom Hardy…the latter is purely all in her mind, but shh don't tell her!

She loves writing angsty, emotionally gripping, sexy romance with passionate alphas and strong-willed women. Her love of reading and writing have always been with her, and while she has a background in certified personal styling, nowadays she's turning her dream of being an author into reality.

She adores all things from the Golden Age of Hollywood, Seinfeld and believes tea is a writing essential. When she isn't writing, she's busy running her own business and spending time with loved ones.

Vanessa loves interacting with readers so please feel free to reach out to her via socials, subscribe to her newsletter, and/or contact her at vanessaluisaauthor@gmail.com for any questions or comments.

Connect with
VANESSA LUISA

Join my Facebook Reader's Group:
www.facebook.com/groups/vanessaluisaslovelies

Subscribe to my MAILING LIST/NEWSLETTER to
be notified of new releases, behind the scenes, and
receive exclusive bonus material:
www.vanessaluisa.com/contact

Instagram: @thevanessaluisa
www.instagram.com/thevanessaluisa

Facebook:
www.facebook.com/vanessaluisaauthor

TikTok: @thevanessaluisa
www.tiktok.com/@thevanessaluisa

Twitter: @thevanessaluisa
www.twitter.com/thevanessaluisa

Follow me on Goodreads:
www.goodreads.com/author/show/21142369.
Vanessa_Luisa

Follow me on Amazon:
www.amazon.com/Vanessa-Luisa/e/B08W1V47PC

Follow me on Pinterest:
www.pinterest.com.au/thevanessaluisa/

Follow me on Spotify:
open.spotify.com/user/itisnessa

Follow me on Bookbub:
www.bookbub.com/authors/vanessa-luisa

Website/Blog: vanessaluisa.com